THE MARK

LEE MOUNTFORD

For my beautiful wife, Michelle. And amazing daughters, Ella and Sophie.

FREE BOOK

Sign up to my mailing list for a free horror book...

Want more scary stories? Sign up to my mailing list and receive your free copy of *The Nightmare Collection - Vol 1* directly to your email address.

This novel-length short story collection is sure to have you sleeping with the lights on.

Sign up now.

www.leemountford.com

1

TONIGHT WAS THE NIGHT.

The man was mentally prepared and ready to go through with what needed to be done, as he had been more than a few times in the past. To say he was used to it, or an expert, would be overstating things, but he was experienced enough to get the job done and leave no trail. At least, he hoped that was the case.

The girl—his target—was oblivious to the pain and torment that was coming for her. After tonight, nothing would be normal for her again. She was doomed.

The small bag the man would take with him was packed —had been for over an hour—and he still had a couple of hours to kill before he needed to depart. So he ran through the upcoming scenario in his mind, playing it over and over, considering any potential problems or unforeseen complications. No matter how much he planned, things were never straightforward. When people were frightened, and fighting for their lives, they were rarely ever predictable. Which meant that his best course of action was to subdue her— and quickly.

The man had considered entering his target's house and waiting inside for her to return, as she was currently out with her friends, though that was not ideal. People on her street were often coming and going, up to the later hours of the evening. Instead, he would wait until she was home and hopefully sound asleep. The girl's neighbours were away, and her house was the last one in the cul-de-sac, so tonight was perfect. After midnight, everything should be quiet.

Gaining entry would be easy. He knew that the girl rarely ever set her alarm when she was home, which was stupid, though he knew the code to disable it should he need to. He also knew what kind of front-door locking mechanism she had installed, and had the required tools in his bag to get past it. So, yes, gaining access was not a problem.

The only problem would be dealing with the girl. There was enough distance to the nearest occupied house that, even if she screamed a little, it should go unnoticed. But if she somehow managed to fight him off and escape, then all of this planning would be for naught.

He could not allow that to happen.

So he waited, patiently, again playing out various scenarios in his mind. In every one, he was successful.

He checked his watch. Still plenty of time, and he actually wished the hours would speed up a little, as he was growing anxious. He just wanted it done now, so he could be free to carry on with his life... for a little while longer, at least.

Another meditative breath.

Soon it would happen. Soon the girl would be marked.

'COME ON,' Amanda said to her, 'it's easy. You've just got to believe in yourself.'

'Easier said than done,' Kirsty replied. 'You've practised this stuff before.'

Her friends laughed as Kirsty readied herself. Amanda stood before her—a rolled-up magazine in hand that doubled as a makeshift knife. Thankfully, other than the four of them, the pub they were in was relatively empty, and the few people that were present were well out of sight, at the main bar around the corner from their little alcove. If Kirsty were to embarrass herself, which she knew she was about to do, at least it would only be in front of friendly company.

'Remember,' Amanda said, 'step into the move. Surprise your attacker and grab my arm at the wrist with both of your hands. Be assertive. Use speed and aggression.'

Peter laughed again from his position at the table. Samantha, his girlfriend, chuckled along with him.

'Do you know how stupid you two look?' Peter asked.

'I don't care, this stuff is important' Amanda told him.

'A few lessons and suddenly Amanda is now Bruce Lee,' Peter commented with a roll of his eyes.

'More than a few lessons,' Amanda told him, before focusing on Kirsty. 'Now, just as we practised. Ready?'

Kirsty was not ready—not at all. They had slowly walked through the move a few times, talking through each of the steps, but Kirsty still had no idea what she was doing. And then, suddenly, Amanda lunged at her, thrusting the rolled-up magazine towards her with more speed than Kirsty was expecting. Kirsty let out a slight shriek and slowly stepped into the move as instructed, reaching for Amanda's wrist, but she was far too slow.

The thrust broke through Kirsty's half-hearted grip and the magazine pressed into her gut.

'You're dead,' Amanda said, not bothering to hide the disappointment in her voice.

'You came at me too quickly!' Kirsty said, as Peter and Samantha rolled around in hysterics.

'Of course I did, otherwise it wouldn't be realistic.' Amanda then held the 'knife' out to Kirsty. 'You attack this time, and I'll show you how it's done.'

'Can't we just sit, talk, and get drunk?' Kirsty asked. 'It's Friday night, and I didn't come out to learn kung-fu.'

'It isn't kung-fu,' Amanda said. 'And we can sit down when we're finished. Now, attack me, like I did to you.'

Knowing that she wouldn't be able to enjoy her night again until they had gone through with the demonstration, Kirsty sighed, took the magazine, and poised herself.

'Ready?' she asked. Amanda just gave her a self-assured smile. Kirsty then thrust her arm forward but, before she knew what was happening, Amanda had her wrist clamped with both hands, exerting surprising force in the process. Kirsty's arm was then quickly and painfully twisted as Amanda ducked under it, and the 'knife' was then thrust back at Kirsty, right into her stomach.

'There,' Amanda said, with a big smile. 'You're dead. Again.'

'Delightful,' Kirsty quipped. 'Can we sit down now?'

Thankfully, Amanda relented, and the two of them joined their friends at the booth. Amanda slid into the booth first and Kirsty shuffled up beside her, before taking a refreshing sip of her gin and tonic. The little exhibition Amanda had put on for them had required a surprising amount of exertion. Peter was right in one sense; Amanda was prone to showing off every now and again, especially with new things she had learned. However, Kirsty knew that there was another reason she had been hauled up to learn these new 'techniques' from her friend. Amanda knew what had happened to her two years ago, and how the mental scars of that ordeal still hadn't healed for Kirsty, and likely never would.

The bar they were in—The Old Lodge—was a large, traditional pub that, back in the day, would have been the kind of place only serious drinkers would frequent. Over the years it had evolved into a more family-friendly place, but the decor—despite being modernised a little—kept its traditional roots. It had a deep red carpet, half-height dark oak panelling on the walls with cream, patterned wallpaper above, and wrought-iron chandeliers dotted across the ceiling.

The four of them—friends from university and now all living in the same town—made an effort to meet up at least once a month. Tonight was one such meet-up, and Kirsty had been looking forward to it, using it as an opportunity to help take her mind off things. But that was ruined when Amanda had announced that she wanted to show off what her new boyfriend—who studied and taught Taekwondo—had shown her. With Amanda being a fitness instructor this new man, whom they had all yet to meet, seemed like a good fit for her. After the announcement, Kirsty had prayed Amanda would pick anyone else for a demonstration, but ultimately she knew the real reason why Amanda was so eager to share the moves, and who she thought needed to know them most.

And that irked Kirsty.

What had happened to her hadn't been some random attack in the street, and certainly not at knifepoint. A man she had once loved—or thought she had loved—had proven to be someone quite different than she thought him to be. While at first Dom was everything she was looking for, over time he had shown his true colours and locked her into a relationship that was mentally abusive.

And then, one night—the worst of her life—the abuse became very much physical.

Kirsty took a longer drink of her gin and savoured the taste. It was her fourth already, two more than anyone else. She was well aware that her friends had noticed this fact, but she liked the feeling it brought—the fuzzy, cloudy feeling that blunted the harsh edges of reality, if only for a little while. Sure, she would regret it in the morning when the hangover kicked in, but at least tonight she could try and forget.

'So,' Samantha said, 'we've seen some of your new fella's fancy moves, thanks to that demonstration. When do we get to meet him?'

'Mike? Not yet,' Amanda stated, swirling the white wine

around in her glass. 'We've just started seeing each other. He has to put in a lot more work until I'm happy that this is serious.'

Peter chuckled, and shook his head. 'Christ, Amanda, you're such hard work. I don't know how you get men to stick around.'

Amanda flashed him a wink. 'Because, I'm the prize, silly.'

Kirsty knew Amanda really believed that, too. And why wouldn't she? The girl was a knockout. While not exactly envious of her, Kirsty could see what men found so attractive about Amanda. For one, thanks to her job, she was in fantastic shape—lean and toned. Her blonde hair was cut into a stylish bob, and her make-up, clothes, and grooming were always immaculate. And, due to the sun-beds she frequented, Amanda was always tanned without letting it go too far—thanks to Kirsty's nagging. When Amanda had first discovered artificial tanning, she was so obsessed that she looked like a dried fruit for a few months, before Kirsty made her see sense. Now her skin tone was a little more natural.

In contrast, Kirsty kept her appearance much more conservative. She still considered herself pretty, just not as glamorous and noticeable as her friend. Kirsty had long, wavy brown hair and big, blue eyes. But she tended to keep her make-up strictly to a little eyeliner, light foundation, and a touch of subtle nail polish when the occasion called for it.

Given their differences, Amanda wasn't the kind of girl Kirsty would normally get along with, and certainly not the type to be her best friend. However, when sharing a room at college, they had clicked, and Kirsty soon saw Amanda for who she really was: a good person, with a good heart, and someone who was loyal and fiercely protective of her friends.

They were so close, in fact, that Amanda was the only person Kirsty had told what had happened to her two years ago. Even Kirsty's parents, whom she loved dearly and who had provided her with everything she could want in life, did not know the truth. They were good people, but she felt that telling them about what had happened would, somehow, change their view of her, make them think less of her. Or pity her.

Amanda had always said that line of thinking was, to quote, *absolute bullshit*, and she was probably right, but Kirsty was still more comfortable with as few people knowing what had happened as possible. And that's why she hadn't gone to the police—another thing that Amanda could never understand. Despite that, and despite Amanda wanting to hunt her ex down and, again to quote, *rip off his balls*, Amanda respected Kirsty's way of handling things.

Well, respected was maybe the wrong phrase. She *accepted* it.

'So how long are you going to keep the poor guy dangling on a hook before you decide what you're doing with him?' Peter asked before taking a sip of his pint of dark ale.

Amanda shrugged. 'I'll know when I know. Until then, he just has to keep dangling.'

'And how about you, Kirsty?' Samantha asked, leaning into Peter a little, with her hand on his knee. These two had gotten together in the last year of university, after a few years of a would-they-wouldn't-they chase, which might sound cute, but for everyone involved it was just annoying. At the time it seemed they were the only people who didn't realise that they would end up together. And, since then, the relationship seemed very strong—to Kirsty, at least. 'Anyone in your life that you aren't telling us about?' Samantha added.

Kirsty took another drink and shook her head. 'Nope,' she said and crunched on an ice cube that had found its way inside of her mouth.

'You're too picky,' Peter said, shaking his head. Kirsty loved both Peter and Samantha, but with them being so settled together, they had an annoying habit of passing judgement on others when it came to relationships, and how easy it was all supposed to be.

'I still don't know why you ever dumped Dom,' Samantha said, and Kirsty tensed up. 'He was gorgeous. And such a nice guy.'

But he wasn't a nice guy. He wasn't a nice guy at all. He was a monster, a fucking wolf in sheep's clothing.

'Kirsty can do better than him,' Amanda said, patting her knee and giving it a subtle squeeze. 'Anyway, fuck men. No offence, Peter. Let's talk about something else.'

Kirsty was more than happy with that, as it was the one topic of conversation that she had little patience for right now. Hell, she would have preferred more of Amanda's self-defence lessons than treading on eggshells while talking about men. She knew that, before long, the line of conversation would circle back to a derivative of *but why did you break up with Dom? He was so nice.* And if she had to go through that one more time, Kirsty thought she would scream. Or cry.

Or both.

Thankfully, with Amanda's pushing, the topic did drift away from men and moved on to more mundane topics such as work, and Peter's bitching about a colleague from the school where he taught.

Kirsty listened as best she could, still riled a little from the mention of Dom, and quickly finished her drink. She then went to order another.

They kept coming, going down very easily, blurring the edges of reality as she had hoped.

As Kirsty continued drinking to forget, she was completely unaware of the terror that awaited.

3

'THANK YOU,' Kirsty said to the taxi driver, trying to keep her words from slurring. She handed the quiet man a ten-pound note. 'Keep the change.' He didn't say anything, merely responding with a grunt. Kirsty shrugged and got out of the taxi, leaving the silent, and rather creepy, driver behind.

The cold night air hit her, quite the contrast from the muggy interior of the car, and Kirsty felt the landscape sway a little due to her inebriated state. Her stomach bubbled, but she successfully fought to keep its contents down. She then approached her front door, fishing the keys from her bag. As she inserted the key into the lock, Kirsty turned again to look at the taxi—which was unmoving, its engine idling. The driver, a big man with pale skin and a thick beard, seemed to be watching her from the side window. Goosebumps formed on her skin and a familiar feeling of anxiety creeped over her.

What was he waiting for?

She had to stop her mind from wandering to a worst-case scenario: the taxi driver getting out of his car, overpowering her, and forcing—

Stop!

There was nothing to get freaked out about here. And then, as if reading her mind, the car pulled forward, turned around in the cul-de-sac just next to Kirsty's house, and drove off. She watched it move down the street, swing around the corner, and disappear from view completely.

She let out a sigh and admonished herself for being overly paranoid. The sound from the distant engine eventually faded to nothing, leaving only silence.

The street—which was comprised of semi-detached properties along one side of the road, the opposite lined with a grass verge and high hedging—was deserted, given the time of night. A couple of lights were on in houses farther up the street, but mostly it seemed like everyone was in bed. It was a quiet area, and Kirsty's house was tucked away at the very end, giving her even more privacy—just as she liked it. But at times like this, when her thoughts got the better of her, she wished there was a little more noise or human interaction.

Kirsty finished unlocking the front door and entered her house, back into the welcome warmth. While her house was hardly new, it was one she loved and was proud of, having made it her own since moving in. Adding her own stamp and spending quite a lot of money on it. Still, if her father was to be believed, she had spent the money in the wrong areas. *Surface level stuff*, he had called the changes. Apparently, Kirsty should have focused on the essentials, like replacing the front and rear doors, which still had old-style locks that, if secured, needed a key to unlock from the inside. Or even swapping out the upstairs windows, which at present weren't large enough to escape from in the event of a fire. Upon his first visit her father had even commented on the poor state of the heating system. All of these points Kirsty had said she would get around to, but never did.

She kicked off her boots and left them haphazardly in the small entrance lobby, continuing straight ahead, passing the stairs, to the kitchen. Kirsty dropped her purse onto the breakfast bar and keys onto the countertop and ran herself a large glass of cold water from the tap, gulping it down in three large mouthfuls.

She let the liquid churn in her gut for a moment, again struggling to keep from retching as the alcohol in her system filled her with nausea. Kirsty knew she should eat something, to help soak up the liquor in her system, but she just didn't have the energy to prepare anything. Instead, she dropped the glass into the sink and peered out the kitchen window before her, into the back garden that was surrounded by a high fence. The garden was engulfed in shadow and, as Kirsty continued to stare, she had visions of something stepping forward from the darkness.

No, not something. *Someone.*

But no one came. She was scaring herself again, unnecessarily. She shook her head in an effort to clear it, and walked from the kitchen, her socked feet padding across tiles that felt cool beneath her. She stopped at the front door and debated whether or not to put on the alarm, at least to the entrance area. But the system, if she was honest, confused her, and had ever since that odd guy who installed it had first explained it to her. She knew how to set it when she left the house, as that was just activating the full system, but having all the zones on in the night would be of no use, because if she moved upstairs then that would set everything off. It was separating out the various areas that she wasn't comfortable with, scared she would make a mistake and end up with the alarm blaring during the night. Instead, she double-checked the lock and —when satisfied it was secure—made her way upstairs, the timber boards underfoot creaking as usual as she went.

Kirsty brushed her teeth and gargled mouthwash, knowing full well that her mouth would still taste like a garbage bin come the morning. She then used the toilet and shuffled off to her bedroom.

Her room was a large one, with fitted wardrobes, a seated vanity area, and a queen-sized bed. Of all the spaces in the house, this room was by far her favourite. It felt like a place just for her, somewhere she could retreat from the world. And this bedroom, unlike the one in her last house, had not been sickeningly soiled.

She stripped herself of her clothing, but, too tired to even throw them in the hamper, dropped them to the floor, then slipped under the crisp, cool sheets. It didn't take her long to fall into a deep, if troubled, sleep.

She was in her home. Her old home.

The weather was gorgeous outside, and she'd spent every second of the day with Dom.

It had been horrible.

Dom used to be the guy Kirsty pictured when planning her future. She would imagine herself wrapped up in his strong arms, looking up at his big smile, and they would be laughing as their baby crawled around before them, cooing and playing. But things had changed, and now she just wanted to be away from him. He wasn't the same person anymore.

Or, rather, she was beginning to see who the real Dom was.

Controlling, hurtful, and possessive.

Dom had just asked for a sandwich, which she was dutifully making for him in the kitchen. Then, suddenly, her surroundings morphed; it was night, and they were up in her bedroom. Dom was horny, but Kirsty was tired and had a headache.

At least, that's what she told him.

Truth was, he was beginning to make her skin crawl. She did not want to be with him. She had to tell him, to put an end to it, as she needed to be free again. But not tonight, not when she was alone with him. That wouldn't end well. She needed to do it somewhere public, so that he wouldn't do anything... stupid.

So, tonight, she would just have to convince him it wasn't going to happen.

'Not tonight, hun. I'm exhausted, and my head is pounding.'

He continued anyway, grabbing the back of her hair and kissing her passionately. She squirmed in his grip, trying to free herself.

'Babe,' she continued, pulling her mouth away. 'Not tonight.'

But he kept going, as if her refusal was something that could be easily overcome or worn down. Or, worse, ignored completely. He grabbed her breast and squeezed it hard, rolling over on top of her. She began to fight now, panicking at what was happening.

'Dom, I said no.'

His hand then moved over her mouth. 'But I want to, so just shut up and put out already.' The calmness with which he said the words terrified her. What *she* wanted meant nothing. In that instant, she felt like an object, not a person. Just a thing, to be used when he had a need for her.

'No!' she shouted.

He curled his lip and struck her.

Then he had his way.

KIRSTY'S EYES sprang open as she panted for breath. Her body was locked rigid, every muscle tense and aching. Sweat coated her brow and her hair was damp and stuck to her skin.

A dream, she said to herself. *It was just a dream.*

She tried to regulate her breathing, to bring her body back under control. Kirsty had had similar dreams before and knew she had to give herself a moment to adjust. Eventually, her muscles relaxed, and her right hand, which she didn't even realise was gripping her covers tightly, relaxed.

She let out a long sigh.

The sheets beneath her felt a little wet, having soaked in her sweat, but she wouldn't get up to change them. Not now. Perhaps in the morning.

A pain in her head suddenly made itself known—an awful, pounding ache that reverberated around her skull. Her mouth was as dry as a desert and swallowing was difficult. This, Kirsty knew, was the hangover she had been hoping she could sleep off.

Just great.

The bedroom was close to pitch black; the only light in the room was from the street light outside, and it crept in from between the small gap in her curtains. She hated the dark, more-so since the incident with Dom, and moved to switch on her bedside light.

Then she stopped, feeling weak and pathetic, like a child —afraid of shadows and monsters under her bed. Granted, the monsters she was afraid of were all too real, but she couldn't let what happened in her past control her like this.

It was like that horrible fucker still had a hold over her. Like he was still winning.

There is no one in this house with you, Kirsty told herself forcefully. *There is no one here who is going to hurt you.*

Then, she heard something from outside her room. At first, she thought it was all in her head, but then she heard it again.

It was unmistakable—a creak on the stairs, as someone slowly made their way up.

Someone was inside the house with her.

4

KIRSTY HELD the covers tight and pulled them up around herself. It felt like a dream, but the adrenaline that now pumped through her veins subdued the pounding headache that only moments earlier had seemed unbearable.

Surely there was no-one outside of her room, on the stairs, creeping up towards her in the dead of night. Surely it was just her imagination, running away with itself after waking from that horrible dream.

She remained deadly silent and listened.

Creak.

Her heart froze in her mouth. This was not the simple moans and groans that a normal home gave off. There was no question now—someone was definitely out there.

Creak.

And whoever it was, they were getting closer, rising up the stairs. Kirsty's mind raced, trying to search out the most appropriate course of action. Her first thought was of the bedroom window, and the possibility of escaping that way: dropping to the floor and outside and taking her chances with the fall. She leaned over in her bed, the mattress squeaking below her, and reached over to pull the curtain back. The windows in the bedroom were big, but the only opening parts to them were too small to fit through. When she had bought the house, the solicitors and her father had raised the point that the windows should be replaced with functional escape ones, and that was something she'd told herself she would get around to, but never had.

And that meant she was trapped in the room.

So what options did that leave? She could possibly yell out, to make it known to whoever was out there that she was awake, and demand to know who it was? Or perhaps run out there to meet them head-on, surprise them with a show of aggression, just as Amanda had recommended.

Whatever Kirsty decided, she knew she couldn't simply wait in place. Her heart pounded in her chest and she had to fight to stop herself from sobbing, so great was the fear that held her in its icy grasp. That same fucking fear had crippled her once before, and her lack of fight then had led to the worst experience of her life.

She couldn't allow that to happen to her again. And yet, she couldn't seem to call her body into action.

Come on, she commanded herself. *Come on!*

Another sound came from the stairway, and Kirsty could tell that whoever was out there was about halfway up, moving slowly, so as not to make too much noise. If that dream hadn't awakened her, she likely wouldn't have heard anything, and would have remained asleep, blissfully unaware of the would-be attacker creeping up on her.

Slowly, Kirsty's shaking body started to reluctantly obey her commands and she sat up, swinging her legs from beneath the covers. Her bare feet lowered and rested on the thick carpet, and Kirsty then gently lifted herself to a standing position. As she did, her bed-frame squeaked loudly.

She stopped dead, her fists clenched, silently cursing the fucking bed for betraying her. Everything in the house was now silent, and she could no longer hear the person outside moving—there was no further creaking of the stairs.

Had they heard her? They had to have. And if so, had they realised that Kirsty was now awake? Or had they taken the noise simply as her adjusting position in bed as she rolled over in her sleep?

That moment—with neither party moving, and Kirsty barely breathing as she was wracked with fear—seemed to last for an eternity. But the moment did end, as she again heard another slow step.

Fuck, fuck, fuck.

Kirsty's heart, already racing, began to beat at an even faster pace. She could wait no more. With every ounce of courage she could muster, Kirsty crept towards the bedroom door and slowly pulled it open.

As she did, she peered out onto the dark landing outside, hoping to see nothing, hoping that the whole experience was just one conjured up by her paranoid, dehydrated mind.

But through the darkness, she could indeed make out a figure coming into view. Its hooded head rose from above the landing bannister. The figure paused, then turned to face her.

She took in a sharp breath.

This person, whoever it was, appeared male, but had covered himself, wrapping some kind of material across his face from the nose down. However, Kirsty did see the glint of the man's eyes, as the two of them stared at each other for a moment.

Kirsty tried to hold it together, tried to be brave, but her worst nightmare was actually coming true. They both remained motionless, and Kirsty let out a low, involuntary sob, sure she was now going to die.

Please, she thought, *just go away. Just leave me alone.*

But he didn't. Instead, the man sprang into action and rushed up the remaining stairs. Kirsty let out a squeal and slammed the door shut, pressing her back forcefully into it after she did, cursing herself for not installing a lock here, and praying she would have the strength to keep the attacker from entering.

As braced as she was, the force at which the stranger crashed into the door rocked her off balance, and she screamed.

'Go away!'

The man did not reply, however, and just continued to push, kick, and heave at the door, trying to force Kirsty back. Kirsty dug her feet in, but the soft carpet afforded her little resistance against the soles of her feet, and, to her horror, she could feel herself sliding forward, inch by inch.

'Please,' she begged, 'just leave me alone!'

But the stranger ignored her and continued his assault. The door was pushed again, revealing a large enough gap for an arm to snake through. Kirsty felt a gloved hand tightly grab her hair, and she shrieked and fought harder, pushing with her legs. It did no good, and the man forced her head forward, pushing her chin down to her chest, then violently and suddenly snapped it back, slamming the back of her skull into the door. Kirsty's hair offered some protection against the blow, but he proceeded to repeat this again and again.

He's going to kill me. I'm going to die here tonight.

Kirsty let herself drop to the floor in the hope of

escaping his grip, but his hold remained firm, even at her lower angle. She shunted herself back against the door, trying to jam his arm in the gap, but soon realised her mistake. Now that she was off her feet, it was much more difficult to hold him at bay, and the door began to slide open more and more. She screamed yet again, but knew now that her efforts were futile. He was going to gain entry, one way or another.

The grip on her hair released as the man seemed to use both hands against the door and it began to open faster, pushing Kirsty back.

With no other option, Kirsty quickly pushed herself to her feet and scrambled over to the other side of the bed, putting it between her and the man, who almost fell into the room.

He stood upright and Kirsty finally got a good look at the stranger. He seemed of average height and of relatively slim build, dressed in dark clothing: cargo trousers, a black hoodie with the hood pulled tight around his head, and a dark scarf or some other garment pulled across his face. She could see his eyes, which glinted blue. On his back he wore a black canvas backpack.

'Please,' she begged again. 'Don't do this. Nothing has happened yet. You can just go. I don't know who you are, or what you want, but you can just walk away. I won't call the police, I swear.'

The stranger stood motionless for a moment with his fists clenched. Was he considering her offer? Was there a chance he would rethink and just turn away?

No.

He answered those questions by launching himself forward and bounding over the bed towards Kirsty. In response, Kirsty lunged to her right, just managing to dodge his outstretched hand. From his higher position on the bed he still had the advantage, and though Kirsty tried to run around the bed to flee the room, he should have been able to cut off her escape route. And he would have, she had no doubt, had the man not lost his footing on the soft mattress. He fell forward and rolled down into the space Kirsty had just occupied, between the bed and the far wall. Kirsty didn't stop to look back and just kept running. She broke through from the room and out onto the landing.

She continued around the bannister and thundered down the stairs, careful not to trip and kill herself in the process of escaping. She leapt down the last three steps and ran to the front door—to freedom—and yanked at the handle.

Locked.

She pulled and heaved, but the door did not budge. She then heard something from behind—a metallic clinking sound. Kirsty slowly turned her head to see the stranger standing at the top of the stairs in the darkness. In his hand, he jangled a set of keys.

Her keys.

The ones, she realised, that she had earlier thrown haphazardly onto the worktop counter in the kitchen, rather than storing them somewhere safe and out of sight. She chastised herself again.

Fuck, fuck, fuck.

Kirsty's would-be attacker then began to make his way down the stairs, carefully, like a hunter creeping towards a nervous deer. And, like a hunted animal, Kirsty bolted, sprinting past the stairs towards the kitchen. As she did, she glimpsed him in her peripheral vision as he vaulted the bannister and dropped down to the floor, landing just behind her.

Kirsty screamed in terror, hoping her voice was loud enough to be noticed by her neighbours. However, with her next-door neighbours away, the sound of her yelling would have to travel even farther to be heard. She scrambled into the kitchen and ran to the island, circling to the back of it as the attacker sprinted into the room behind her.

Her first idea was to run to the glazed door that led from the kitchen to the rear garden, but she knew that it was also locked. The keys were tucked away in one of the kitchen drawers, and she didn't have the time to dig through and find them, so she put the breakfast bar between her and the stranger who was advancing on her.

He came to a stop opposite her, on the other side of the island, and Kirsty could see his blue eyes in more detail now, and they were wide. Not with anger or aggression, however. No, it was more a panicked look, reminiscent of worry or fear. His pale brow was damp with sweat, and she could make out a few strands of mousy hair poking through from under his hood.

'Please,' she said, again, hoping to get through to him. 'Just go. Don't do this.' Kirsty didn't even know what *this* would be, but she knew it would be horrible. And, given that the man actually looked worried, not furious and filled with some kind of sick lust, she couldn't figure out why he wanted to go through with whatever it was.

The stranger standing opposite her then made a slow, deliberate movement as he removed his backpack and rested it on the countertop. He unzipped the top and reached inside, never once taking his eyes off Kirsty.

Kirsty could only watch.

She did think about reaching out to try and snatch the bag away from him, because she knew that whatever he was retrieving would not be anything good. As it was, fear had her rooted to the spot. She saw what he pulled out of the bag, and it made her legs weak.

It was a syringe. Filled with a clear liquid.

'What do you want?' Kirsty shouted, almost tired of being so afraid. The adrenaline that was pumping through her body was beginning to wane now, and a surreal, tired feeling was starting to take over.

Was this it? Was she just accepting defeat, ready to allow this lunatic to do whatever he wanted to her? She remembered having this kind of feeling once before, a submissive impulse, one of pandering to someone who wished to do her harm, in the hope they would reconsider. Or at least go easy on her if she was compliant, like a good little girl. It sickened her to think she could ever feel that way again, especially in the face of such a nightmarish situation. But she was trapped, and she didn't know what else to do.

A random thought popped into her head: a memory of the previous night—the self-defence moves that Amanda had tried to drum into her. Would it help with a man trying to stick her with a needle, filled with who-knows-what? Soon, she had her chance to find out, because the man pounced.

He didn't even try to run around the island, instead opting to vault over it, removing the obstruction between them. Kirsty was stunned and didn't react in time. Amanda had tried to tell her to use aggression to surprise the attacker, to catch them off guard, but she just stood frozen, allowing him to grab her by the throat with his free hand.

This sparked a little more fight in her, but Kirsty soon found herself overpowered. The grip on her throat was stronger than she expected, and she was forced backwards as he slammed her against the glazed double door behind. She half-hoped the force would have been enough to break the glass, and they would have both gone tumbling through into the night outside, perhaps giving her an opportunity to escape. However, the glass in the door was safety glass, and very strong, so her body simply bounced off it as he forced her up against it. Still fighting back, she clawed at his face, dragging her nails at his flesh, but only succeeded in catching the scarf that was covering his face, pulling it down slightly, giving her a look at his long, crooked nose.

And then she felt it, like a scratch, on the side of her neck. She realised where his other hand was—currently plunging the needle into her skin. She cried out and felt the cold, foreign liquid enter her veins as the plunger on the syringe was depressed.

The man then let her go and stepped back.

Kirsty wobbled on her feet and tried to take a step forward, but her legs gave out. She dropped to the floor as a numb feeling washed over her entire body. She remembered feeling vaguely surprised at how quickly that substance—whatever it was—had acted.

No, not like this. Please, God, no.

Her vision started to fade as the drug got to work. From her position—face down on the floor, with her cheek pressed down against the cold tile—she saw her attacker retrieving something else from his bag on the countertop.

Her last vision, before unconsciousness claimed her, was of him pulling free a long, sharp knife.

5

HE STOOD over the girl's prone body, breathing heavily. That had not gone to plan. Had she not heard him and woken up, he was certain things would have gone smoothly. Instead, she had made a lot of noise before he'd managed to subdue her. He could only hope that her screaming and yelling hadn't attracted attention, because what he needed to do next would take a little time. It was intricate work and he needed to use care and patience.

The procedure—if that was the right word for it—consisted of two stages. The first was to prepare the girl, making sure she was physically ready for what was about to enter her. That involved cutting her. The second step would complete the ritual, and it was at that time he had to be careful and precise—to make sure that he left no DNA behind.

He looked over the knife, the one he had taken from that place many years ago when he had escaped. It was ceremonial, with a golden handle engraved with specific markings. Whether it was critical for what he was doing, or if any object capable of cutting would do, he wasn't certain. He didn't think it mattered, but he had never taken the chance or felt the need to find out.

The man set the knife down beside the girl, one he found quite attractive. But girlfriends and relationships were not for him. His life, such as it was, wouldn't allow it. He hated that he was denied such normal things—experiences that others took for granted.

But that was the way of things. This was his curse.

The closest, most intimate encounters he'd ever had with women were all like this. Always when they were unconscious, after he had drugged them. Well, not always after they were drugged, as during his first few times they had to be knocked out in more... violent... ways; but he had learned to improve his process, which made things less unpredictable for him.

Not that tonight had shown any of those improvements. The man thought he had been quiet when ascending the stairs. Sure, there was a little noise as he moved, but he hadn't thought it enough to wake anyone who was sleeping soundly. But then she had opened the bedroom door, and looked out, catching him in the act. Then it had all gone to shit.

The man now reached down and pulled up the girl's t-shirt, lifting it high up above her sky-blue pajama bottoms, revealing the flesh of her back. She had relatively pale skin —though not as pale as his own—that looked almost unblemished. Two dimples just above her buttocks were the only things that stood out, and he found them endearing, though he wasn't certain why. His thoughts ran to more animalistic urges, of what he could do to her in this situation... but he fought the impulses back, feeling disgusted in himself. In any case, giving in to his lust would ruin everything.

And it would only make him more of a monster... if that were possible. What he was about to do to the girl was bad enough.

Worse, in fact.

He picked up the knife and moved it towards the flesh of his victim.

6

KIRSTY WAS WITH DOM AGAIN—IN her old bedroom, cowering in the corner—as he stood over her with a self-satisfied grin on his face.

'I'm ready to go again,' he said and grabbed his crotch through his underwear.

'I don't want to,' Kirsty replied, her voice sounding soft and echoey, like it was coming through from a great distance.

It sounded weak, even to Kirsty.

'Well, that doesn't really matter, does it?'

Dom reached for her and grabbed her by the shoulders. Kirsty made a meek mewling sound in protest, but felt herself lifted up with little effort, as if she had no weight to her. She was brought up to his face and looked into his eyes.

Something wasn't right.

The irises weren't his usual brown, but rather a stark yellow with flecks of green. The pupils were a deep black, but they were tiny, like pinpricks, and the normal whites of the sclera were now a blood-red. His smile widened, revealing rows of razor-sharp teeth.

'*You are mine now, bitch,*' he said in a voice that was not his own. It sounded wrong, not human, more... demonic.

A laugh echoed from him, and he spun Kirsty around, pushing her up to the window. The view outside was not one she remembered. Indeed, the normal landscape she recalled from the house had been replaced by something else entirely. A hellscape.

A place not of this world.

The sky was filled with alien stars that swirled high above a black, rocky landscape. The pulsating stars seemed to move far too quickly, drifting together to form something akin to a horrible, watching eye. Obsidian towers, dizzying in height, broke from the ground and speared up into the air. Terrifying demons, some as tall as mountains, stalked the horrible new world.

Was this hell?

'*Worse than hell,*' Dom said, as if reading her thoughts. Kirsty felt his large hands—with long, claw-like fingers—grab hold of her head, engulfing her cranium in his grip.

He then squeezed, and Kirsty felt her skull begin to crack. She let out a scream.

KIRSTY WAS STILL YELLING, kicking, and flailing as she came to and realised that she had been dreaming.

She wasn't in that room, in Dom's grasp, staring out over a hellish vista. Rather, she was still on her kitchen floor, where she'd been when she passed out.

The dream had been terrifying—real and raw—like she could actually feel the pressure from Dom's grip on her skull, and even smell the sulfurous odour of his breath. She rolled to her side, panting, still scared by the vision.

It was just a dream. There's nothing to be scared of.

Then the memory of *why* she found herself unconscious on the kitchen floor came flooding back to her, and she realised that there was indeed a reason to be scared. Kirsty hadn't just passed out, she had been drugged. Flashbacks of the attack hit her like a solid wall of fear and desperation: of waking up and seeing that man on the stairs. Him rushing her before she escaped down the stairs. The way he jingled the keys, almost mocking her. Then the stand-off in the kitchen, where she saw the look of apprehension in his blue eyes as he drew out the syringe. The aggression as he overpowered her and stuck her with the needle. And lastly, the knife.

Panic gripped Kirsty, and she pushed herself up to a sitting position. She tasted copper in her mouth. Had she cut her gums or tongue? Light poured into the room from the windows and glazed door to the garden, indicating night had passed. But did that mean her attacker had fled?

It was then the pain in Kirsty's back made itself known: a sharp, stinging sensation. She reached her hand around to the lower section of her back as best she could and felt something rough and crusty to the touch. She then brought her hand back around and looked to her fingers, seeing dried blood smeared on them. Then her eyes were drawn to the floor below her, and she saw a few streaks of the flaky brown substance on the tile as well.

What the hell had he done to her?

She looked around the room, frantic, her head swivelling in quick motions as she nervously tried to pick up any signs of her attacker. There was no one else here in the kitchen, at least, but perhaps he was elsewhere in the house, just waiting for her to wake so that he could torment her further? Logically, she knew that probably wasn't the case, given that she had been unconscious for so long. So it was likely that the fucker had done whatever he'd intended—whatever that was—and fled before she had come to. But Kirsty wasn't really thinking logically; she was beyond terrified. A nightmare scenario had just come to pass—she had been attacked again, overpowered, used, and left feeling pathetic and helpless. All these years since Dom's violation of her spent thinking the boogeyman was still hiding in the shadows, waiting to pull her back into that feeling of helplessness, turned out to be true.

There had indeed been a boogeyman waiting for her, and in her own home, to boot.

Kirsty slowly got to her feet. She felt like hell: nauseous, dizzy, and her lower back seemed as though it was on fire. She listened, but could hear nothing—no movement, no breathing, no sign of anybody else. Looking to the clock on the microwave, she saw that it was a little before nine in the morning. She had been unconscious for a while, leaving her attacker enough time to do whatever the hell he wanted to her. Running a finger over her gums and tongue, Kirsty could find no sign of injury, no soreness, but a taste of blood was definitely there.

She needed to call the police—unlike last time, with Dom, when she really should have but didn't. Kirsty knew that staying silent on the attack now was just not an option. Her mobile phone was upstairs, on her bedside table—as long as her attacker hadn't stolen it—but there was a land-line handset in the living room. She just had to walk through there and pick it up. But the thought of doing that simple task scared the hell out of her. She felt sure that the second she walked out of the kitchen the man would be there, waiting for her—hood pulled tight, a scarf covering his face revealing only those wide, blue eyes.

Ready to attack again.

She gave herself a moment, then pushed the fear down. With slow and steady steps, she made her way through to the entrance lobby. The front door was closed. Not broken, not smashed, and not in any way disturbed. She tentatively gripped the handle and pulled at it.

Locked. As it had been last night when she had tried to escape.

And the last time she had seen the keys, they had been dangling from her attacker's fingers as he stood at the top of the stairs. God only knew where they were now.

Kirsty poked her head into the living room, checking to see that it was empty. The notion that the man was well-and-truly gone was now starting to seem real, but there was always that nagging doubt. The coast was clear, so she ran to the phone on the side table next to the sofa and snatched up the receiver. She half expected the line to be dead but, thankfully, Kirsty heard the dial tone. Before she dialled, however, Kirsty looked to the far wall where a thin but full-length mirror hung. She looked at her reflection and hated what she saw.

She looked like hell.

But worse than that, she looked terrified and scared, and she fucking hated that.

Trying to hold back the tears, Kirsty punched in the emergency services number and hit connect. After a few rings, someone answered.

'Which service do you require?' A female voice asked.

'I... I need help,' Kirsty replied. 'I've been attacked. In my home. I was knocked out. Please help.'

'Okay, I'll put you through to the police,' the lady said. Kirsty was then transferred, and another voice, again female, answered.

'Police emergency.'

'I need help,' Kirsty said again and felt a well of emotion come pouring out. She began to sob. 'Someone broke into my home last night. They attacked me. Drugged me. I've just woken up. I don't know what...' she broke down.

'Okay,' the female voice replied in a calm but assertive tone. 'Tell me where you are.'

'I'm at home,' Kirsty said.

'What's the address?' Kirsty gave her address, and the woman on the other end of the phone went on. 'Are you safe?'

'I don't know. I don't know if he's still here,' Kirsty said, keeping her voice as low as possible. She didn't think he was, but couldn't be certain, and she was terrified that he might be.

'Can you get somewhere secure? Is there a bathroom where you can lock yourself inside?'

Kirsty thought about that, knowing the only bathroom was on the floor above. 'I'd need to go upstairs, and I don't know where he is.'

'Okay,' the lady replied, 'try and hide somewhere in the room you are in. Don't worry, the police are on their way to you now. What's your name?'

Kirsty moved over to her couch and ducked down beside the arm closest to the far wall, wedging herself into the limited space. It wasn't much of a hiding spot, but it was the best one available.

'It's Kirsty,' she replied, 'Kirsty Thompson.'

'Thank you, Kirsty. Can you hear anything? Someone moving around in the house?'

Kirsty listened, but other than the birds outside and the sound of someone cutting their grass, there was nothing.

'No,' Kirsty replied. 'I can't.'

'Okay. Just stay where you are. Can you remember what happened?'

'I woke up last night and I heard someone in the house, on the stairs. When I looked out of my bedroom, there was a man. I didn't see his face, he was wearing a hood, but he came at me. I tried to get away, and managed to get downstairs, but he caught me. Then he stuck me with a needle. I passed out and only woke up a few minutes ago. I think he's done something to me. My back has been bleeding, and it's painful.'

'Are you injured?' the woman asked, still maintaining a calm tone, which actually helped keep Kirsty from falling apart entirely.

'I think so.'

'Okay, then I'll send an ambulance as well.'

'Thank you.'

'The police are nearly with you, Kirsty, but I'll stay on the line until they get there.'

True to her word, the woman on the other end of the line did stay with Kirsty, but a few minutes later there was a banging on the front door. Kirsty jumped and yelled out in fright. She could see the front door from her vantage point and could make out blurred figures through the opaque glass panel.

'What's wrong, Kirsty?' the female voice asked.

'A bang,' she replied. 'There was a bang on the front door. Someone's here.'

'Yes, it's the police.'

Kirsty felt a wave of relief. 'The door is locked,' she said. 'I don't know where the keys are.'

'That's okay,' the woman said, and Kirsty heard quick typing on a keyboard from the other end of the line. 'Stay where you are, and don't approach the door. They are coming in.'

And come in they did, as a few moments later there was a thunderous crash against the front door. Then another. And another.

Finally, the door swung inward, and two people entered. A tall, broad man in police uniform was the first to appear, and he was carrying a heavy-looking metal battering ram, painted red. This man was followed by another officer—a woman, who was not much shorter than he was.

'Are the police with you, Kirsty?' the woman on the other end of the phone asked.

'Yes,' Kirsty said, feeling that wave of relief again. She began to cry. 'They're here.'

'It's okay, Kirsty. I'll let you go and speak to them.'

Kirsty slowly got to her feet, and the female officer looked over to her.

'Are you Kirsty?' the officer asked.

Kirsty nodded as the tears streamed down her face. 'Please... help me.'

7

POLICE CONSTABLE ERIN JONES walked over to Kirsty Thompson, the girl who had called in the report of an attack, who was currently squatted down beside the sofa. Kirsty appeared shaken and ashen—a look Erin had seen before when being called out to incidents like this. The woman's long, dark hair was frazzled, and dark bags hung under her tear-filled eyes. Erin noticed a smear of dried blood across the fingers of the woman's left hand as she reached up to grab the arm of the couch.

'It's okay, Kirsty,' Erin said, approaching the sobbing girl. Kirsty tentatively stepped out from her position next to the sofa, hugging herself. Erin felt her partner's presence loom from behind as Officer Edwards moved to stand next to her, having set down 'the big red key,' as it was known. Erin turned to him and spoke quietly. 'Are you okay looking around here on your own? I'll speak to the victim.'

Edwards nodded. 'No problem.'

The tall man then took out his extendable steel baton, and, with a flick of his wrist, popped it out to its fullest length. He walked from the room, heading out to tour the ground floor. Erin didn't like sending him off on his own, given that securing the property really should be a two-person job, but they couldn't leave the victim alone while they did that, and the two of them were the only officers present. Until the ambulance showed up, they would have to deal with this situation on their own and secure the premises.

Edwards was capable, however, and his intimidating size was usually enough to deter anyone from trying anything stupid. And if they did try something, then Erin was more than capable of helping out. But given the briefing Dispatch had relayed—that the girl had been attacked the previous night—Erin had a feeling that the house would be empty. Especially as the girl had been free to lodge the call for help this morning. There was little chance the perpetrator was still around, as they surely wouldn't have allowed that to happen.

The thought of what this girl had been through turned Erin's stomach, but she had to stay focused and professional.

'Someone attacked me,' the girl said. 'I don't know who. I couldn't get a good look, but when I woke up last night, I saw him on my stairs. I tried to get away, but he caught me in the kitchen. He... he drugged me. Then did something to me while I was unconscious. I don't know what, but I know he did something.'

It was like a stream of consciousness verbally pouring itself out of the girl. As if she needed to express everything quickly, to make sure she got it out, but there was a tentativeness there as well—a reluctance, like she was unsure Erin would believe her story. Another thing that Erin hated about calls like this.

Erin walked up to Kirsty and gestured to the sofa. 'It's okay,' she said again. 'Please, sit down.' The girl did, perching on the front edge of the sofa, and Erin noticed that she winced as she did. Something else caught Erin's attention as well: a stain, dark brown, coating the rear of the woman's t-shirt. She knew what it was—blood that had soaked through the material.

'Okay, Kirsty, I want you to tell me everything you remember. But I also just want to check something. Can I lift up your t-shirt?' she asked, and Kirsty nodded. 'I'm going to need you to stand up again.'

The girl complied. 'Something on my back stings,' she said. 'I'm not sure what has happened.'

Erin heard Edwards' footsteps come back into the entrance hallway, and she turned to see him stand in the doorway, his large frame dominating the opening.

'Kitchen is clear,' he said. 'I'll check upstairs.'

Erin nodded, and Edwards ascended the stairs, his footsteps sounding heavy as he went. Erin then turned her attention back to Kirsty and gently lifted up the girl's t-shirt, revealing what was beneath. Erin could see clearly what had happened, and the source of Kirsty's pain. But, in all her years of being on the beat, Erin had never seen anything quite like this before.

The girl had been cut, in a very deliberate way.

Upon seeing the wounds, Erin was unable to hide her surprised intake of breath that she drew in.

'What is it?' Kirsty asked, worried.

Erin didn't know how to respond.

EDWARDS SEARCHED the upper floor of the property thoroughly, as he had the ground floor, but found nothing—no sign of intruders. A full inspection of the property, by the forensics team, would determine if there was anything here they could use to catch their man, but there was really nothing else for him to see.

And Edwards really hoped they found their man, because the thought of freaks like this getting away with what they had done sickened him.

It happened far too often, to the extent that Edwards wondered how much of a difference he actually made, doing what he did. All of the work he put in, all of the compiling of evidence to form a case, only to have it completely fall away for the slightest mistake or technicality. And seeing the vile humans they were trying to put away strut free time after time... it sometimes made him think it would be easier—and more just—if he could just get a few hours alone in a room with these people.

No cameras. No holding back.

Only the punishment that these people deserved.

He had—half-jokingly—posed the idea to Erin once, and she had told him, in no uncertain terms, how stupid the notion was. But not before finishing with: 'Besides, if we could get away with that kind of thing, then you would have to get in line behind me.'

He believed that, too. Edwards had seen how Erin handed herself in difficult situations, and he'd learned a lot from her in doing so. She didn't have his size—though, at five-foot-nine, she was hardly short—but she didn't need it. She had speed and a surprising amount of controlled aggression.

Edwards made his way back downstairs, just in time to see the ambulance pull up outside. He looked into the living room and saw Erin and the victim still in there, and Erin was examining an apparent injury on the girl's lower back, though he couldn't make out exactly what it was. He wanted to go and find out a little more, but Erin had it covered, so he waited for the two paramedics as they entered through the open door, both men donning green overalls. He stepped aside and let them enter.

'What have we got?' the older of the two asked.

'A girl, mid-to-late twenties, I'd estimate. She woke up last night to find an intruder in her house. She was attacked, and, we think, drugged. No one else is here now, so the place is secure.'

He followed the two paramedics into the living room. They rushed over to Kirsty, and Erin stepped aside. Edwards noticed that Erin looked a little... off. Not exactly shaken, but not her normal self, either. Something had bothered her. Erin stepped towards him as the paramedics tended to the girl.

'What's up?' Edwards quietly asked.

'That fucker,' Erin spat, 'whoever he was. He cut something into her back. A symbol.'

'What do you mean?' Edwards asked, giving her a confused look.

'Exactly what I said,' she replied. 'An honest-to-God symbol or something, like some kind of ritualistic thing. It's like she's been fucking branded.'

Erin rarely swore, especially on duty.

Edwards looked over to the girl, who was becoming increasingly distressed. He saw the paramedics looking over the injury, and could make out a little of the detail through the flakey, dried blood.

'Jesus,' he exclaimed.

～

'WHAT IS IT?' Kirsty asked, desperate to know what everyone was keeping from her. The female police officer had seen something on her back, the cause of the stinging pain, Kirsty assumed, but before things had been explained, the paramedics had arrived and were now looking over what she assumed was a wound.

The female police officer's initial reaction at seeing whatever it was—that sharp intake of breath—bothered Kirsty.

But no one seemed very eager to fill her in on the situation.

What had the attacker done to her last night?

'It's okay, miss,' one of the paramedics said. 'You have some cuts on your back. We will treat them as best we can here, but we might need to get you to a hospital.'

'What kind of cuts?' Kirsty pressed. Surely a few simple cuts wouldn't have caused the reaction Kirsty had witnessed. She'd even overheard the large policeman utter 'Jesus Christ' a few moments ago.

'Until we treat them, it's hard to say,' the paramedic replied, but Kirsty detected a certain reluctance in his voice. If he wasn't outright lying, then he was definitely holding something back.

'No!' Kirsty shouted. 'There's something you aren't telling me. What the hell did he do to me?'

'Kirsty,' the female officer cut in and walked back over. 'We need you to calm down. Let the paramedics do their job and check you over.'

'No!' Kirsty yelled again. Only this time, she jumped up to her feet. 'Tell me what's going on. Now.'

'Please,' the female officer said, but Kirsty didn't want to hear it, and she turned and walked past the police, and paramedics, to the full-length mirror that was mounted on the far wall. She held up her top and turned around to see for herself.

It took a few moments for her to make sense of what it was she was seeing. Then, it started to come together, and as it did, she felt as if she was going to pass out. Her knees gave way, but before she could fall she felt the female police officer's arms around her, propping her up.

'What did he do?' Kirsty wailed. 'What did he fucking do to me?'

'It's okay,' the officer said. 'It's going to be okay.'

But how could it be okay? If that thing left a scar, then Kirsty was going to be branded for life.

Crudely carved, she could make out two concentric circles with strange markings between, and an inverted triangle inside the inner ring. It was a symbol, one that looked distinctly occult-like, and it had been etched into Kirsty's flesh.

8

KIRSTY WAS DRESSED in a dingy blue disposable gown as a nurse scrapped a small wooden stick under her fingernails, collecting any evidence that that may be hidden there.

The room they were in was a small one, with a single bed, but Kirsty was thankful for the privacy. The walls had once been white here, but had faded over time, and not been given the update they so desperately needed. The same could be said for the rest of the hospital that she had seen on her way to this room. The whole place seemed so... worn.

When she arrived, that horrible disfigurement on her back had been quickly and efficiently cleaned and dressed by a stern-looking middle-aged nurse, one who reminded Kirsty more of a strict teacher than someone in the caring profession. The nurse had introduced herself as Audrey and informed Kirsty that she was a Sexual Offences Examiner—and would be carrying out a forensic medical examination.

Another person soon joined them—a policewoman—just before Nurse Audrey had started scraping beneath

Kirsty's fingernails. This lady introduced herself as Officer Ansari, and she was a SOIT Officer—a Sexual Offences Investigative Trained Officer.

The Asian lady had a kind face, almost the polar opposite of Nurse Audrey, and soon began asking Kirsty to recount as much as she could remember about the attack. Kirsty did just that and went over everything yet again, hating every second of having to re-live it.

The whole experience, of being examined and questioned, felt surreal, almost dream-like. Kirsty wasn't sure if it was a case of the adrenaline finally wearing off, or finally being able to feel some measure of security now that she was in a safe environment. Regardless, she suddenly felt drained and lightheaded. Perhaps it was shock?

Nurse Aubrey then began to swab the insides of Kirsty's mouth, and Kirsty felt the soft bud of the stick press firmly into the inside of her cheek before it was pulled around the rest of her mouth. The swab was bagged up as evidence, as were the sticks that had been jabbed beneath her fingernails. The whole thing felt mildly embarrassing, but Kirsty was just too tired to really care.

Nurse Aubrey then explained, in a matter-of-fact tone, that the examination would now need to get a little more... personal, and asked if Kirsty was okay with that. Kirsty just nodded and tried to switch off her mind as she lay back on the bed and allowed her gown to be lifted up.

～

'WHAT THE FUCK?'

Amanda's voice on the other end of the line was loud and thick with anger. So much so that Kirsty moved the mobile phone away from her ear a little. 'When?' Amanda went on. 'How? What the fuck happened? Who the fuck did this to you? I'll rip their balls off!'

Kirsty had called her friend and told her about what had happened the previous night, and Amanda's reaction had been as expected. Kirsty loved her a little bit for that.

Kirsty knew that she had to tell someone about the incident, and while her parents may have been the obvious choice, she felt that same sense of misplaced guilt as she had when Dom had attacked her.

No, he didn't just attack you. He raped you.

She hated keeping her parents out of something like this, but, yet again, she didn't want them to look at her any differently. So, Amanda was the only choice she had. Yet again, her friend was the only person Kirsty felt she could really trust.

After going over the story of what happened, Amanda asked if Kirsty needed anything from her.

'Well, the nurse said I could spend the night here, which is good,' Kirsty said, 'because I really don't want to have to go back home on my own. Would you be able to pick me up sometime tomorrow?'

'Of course,' Amanda said. 'I had some classes scheduled, but I can easily rearrange them.'

'Oh, if it's going to be a bother...'

'No, it's no bother, Kirsty, I'm coming to get you. And I'll stay with you tomorrow and spend the night as well, just so you aren't alone.'

'You don't have to,' Kirsty said, not really meaning it. The truth was, Amanda's offer was one that she really wanted to take, as the idea of spending the night alone in her own house filled her with dread.

'I won't take no for an answer,' Amanda said as if reading Kirsty's mind, and Kirsty felt a wave of relief wash over her.

'Well, in that case, sounds good.'

There was a slight pause before Amanda asked, 'So, how are you doing?'

'I'm okay,' Kirsty replied. 'I should have paid more attention to your self-defence class, though.' Kirsty laughed as she spoke, but even to her the laugh sounded empty and forced.

'Kirsty, be honest with me.'

'I feel like hell,' Kirsty admitted. 'And the worst thing is, other than waking up to find his little calling card cut into my skin, I have no idea what he did to me after he drugged me.'

'Have the doctors said anything?'

'The nurse said she couldn't see any obvious signs of sexual assault, but they've taken samples that will be sent off to be tested and used as evidence. Even then, she said that they might not find anything.'

'So, are they going to catch the fucker?'

'I don't know,' Kirsty said. 'Depends what evidence the investigation turns up. I don't know that they have anything to go on so far.'

'They better catch him!' Amanda said, raising her voice. 'He can't get away with this. It's not fair!'

'I know,' Kirsty agreed. 'But he might.'

'He fucking won't,' Amanda stated. 'I'll find him myself if I need to.'

This brought a genuine laugh from Kirsty. 'I bet you would.' There was then another silence between them. 'I'm scared,' Kirsty admitted. 'It's like it's happening all over again. First with Dom, and now...'

'You are going to be okay,' Amanda told her. 'It's okay to be scared, but you are strong enough to get through this. Strong enough to get through anything. I'm telling you, hun, it's going to be okay.'

'I guess,' Kirsty said, without really believing it. Though she did appreciate Amanda's efforts to raise her spirits.

'It will be,' her friend re-affirmed.

The tiredness Kirsty felt earlier was growing, making her eyelids heavy. She yawned.

'Am I that boring?' Amanda asked.

'I'm just exhausted,' Kirsty replied. 'I feel like I could sleep for a week.'

'Then do just that. Or at least until I pick you up tomorrow.'

'I might.'

'Okay, I'll let you go. Sleep well, Kirsty, and I'll see you tomorrow.'

'Okay, bye,' Kirsty said. 'And Amanda... thank you.'

'No problem,' Amanda replied, then ended the call.

The talk with Amanda had actually helped to lift Kirsty's spirits a little, though she still felt terrible. She wanted to just lie down and go to sleep, but the pressure on her bladder meant that would be impossible until she had visited the bathroom, and she wasn't sure exactly where that was. However, with immaculate timing, a portly nurse entered the room.

'Just collecting the rubbish,' the nurse said, retrieving the empty plastic plate and glass from Kirsty's side table. 'How was it?'

The nurse was referring to the meal Kirsty had eaten, which consisted of chicken, mashed potato, peas, and gravy. In truth, the food was tolerable, but no better than that.

However, Kirsty had been so hungry she had devoured the entire dish in a matter of minutes.

'It was nice,' Kirsty said, telling a little white lie.

'Glad to hear,' the nurse replied.

'Can you tell me where the toilet is?' Kirsty asked. 'I was shown, but have completely forgotten.'

'That's okay, my dear, this place can be a little bit of a rabbit warren. I'm heading past it now, actually, so you can just follow me if you'd like?'

'Sounds good.'

Kirsty rolled herself from the bed, feeling the sting of the wound on her back as she did, and stood to her feet. Her legs felt tingly as the blood again began to flow, following hours of just lying in bed. She took a step, getting the feeling back, and then another. Then she noticed a confused and startled expression on the nurse's face.

'What is it?' Kirsty asked, following the woman's gaze, realising she was looking beneath the bed.

'I swear I just...' The nurse didn't finish, but instead walked past Kirsty, over to the bed. She lifted the sheets that hung over the side, revealing the dark space beneath the metal-framed bed. It was empty.

'What?' Kirsty asked again, feeling a little freaked out.

The nurse just gave an embarrassed laugh. 'I think my old eyes are playing tricks on me,' she said. 'I could have sworn I saw something under there.'

'Something?'

The nurse shook her head. 'It was nothing, obviously. I think I'm just working too hard. Come on, I'll show you to the toilet.'

Kirsty followed the nurse from the room, but not before glancing back at the bed, confused as to what the nurse thought she had seen.

NURSE GRACE NORMAN WAS TIRED. That was the only explanation for it.

She was nearing the end of a thirteen-hour shift, which had followed baby-sitting a grouchy granddaughter for four hours. Her feet were aching, and she was ready to go home and soak in a hot bath.

So she had put what she thought she had seen down to pure exhaustion.

In all her years here, Grace had seen many strange things. And more than once in the hospital, she had felt as if some unseen presence was sharing a space with her, watching. It was a feeling that someone else was there, someone unseeable, and, given that the hospital had seen a lot of people pass to the next life, it made sense to her that some people hung about a little bit longer after death. Many of her friends mocked her for her beliefs, but Grace didn't mind. Her faith was her faith.

However, despite the feelings and weird experiences she'd had over the years, never once had she actually seen anything with her own eyes.

Until now, that was. But it couldn't have been real.

Just before taking the young girl, Kirsty, to the toilet, something had caught her eye. Then, after escorting the girl back, and tucking her in to get some sleep, Grace had checked again.

But she had found nothing.

And Grace had even returned to the room—just before her shift ended—to see Kirsty soundly asleep in her bed. But, again, nothing under the bed. So Grace had pulled closed the room's privacy curtain around the bed and left Kirsty to her slumber before clocking off for the day.

But even on the drive home, Grace still couldn't shake what she thought she had seen, if only for a moment, partially masked by the overhanging sheets.

A female figure had been lying beneath the bed, wide-eyed, and staring back at her.

9

KIRSTY AWOKE IN ANOTHER PANIC, swimming in sweat.

She knew immediately that she had been dreaming, but, like the previous night, the nightmare had seemed very real. And very, very scary. It had again started with Dom, but quickly shifted to that strange... *otherplace*... again. An almost-alien world filled with horrors Kirsty could scarcely believe her mind had conjured up.

It took a few moments of panting as she lay in her bed, but the terror locked in her chest started to subside, and she eventually remembered where she was: still alone in the private hospital room. Perfectly safe.

Though, if she were honest with herself, she didn't feel particularly safe and hadn't since the night of the attack. Perhaps that was natural, considering what had happened, but Kirsty couldn't shake the feeling that she was constantly being watched. Even now, in the dark room—illuminated only by the light that came in from the hallway outside—she could feel unknown eyes on her. The feeling was perhaps made worse by the curtain pulled around the bed, making Kirsty feel even more enclosed. She could see nothing beyond the dull white curtain, save for the muted splash of light from the corridor that pushed its way through the thin material. There was a window to her left, on the external wall, and the blinds were pulled closed, not allowing any of the glow from the moon to creep through.

Kirsty listened, hearing faint voices outside in the hall-way, as well as the occasional squeak of footsteps on the linoleum floor as people passed, going about their business. She retrieved her phone from the bedside table and checked the time. The back-lit screen came to life, causing her to squint, and showed it was just now three a.m. Kirsty set the phone down again and dropped her head back to her pillow, which felt damp beneath her neck. Before initially going to sleep, she'd pulled her hair up into a bun, but it was currently doing little to cool her.

She took a breath. Her mind was now far too alert to fall back to sleep, so her two options were to either occupy herself on her mobile phone, or just lie there and wait for her mind to settle and hope she could get some more sleep before the morning came. Given that she didn't have her phone charger with her, and knowing how exhausted she would be tomorrow with no rest, she decided the second option was the more sensible one, and so she closed her eyes and concentrated on her breathing.

A couple of people outside passed her room. She heard their voices chatting, and their footsteps as they walked. Even with her eyes closed, she could detect the brief drop in light as their bodies moved in front of her door and blocked the hallway's glow.

The noise wasn't particularly intrusive or loud, but she found herself focusing on it, instead of allowing her mind to rest. After a few moments, the light level dulled again, but there were no footsteps accompanying any passersby this time. And the feeling of a shadow blocking the light did not disappear.

Kirsty opened her eyes and turned her head.

She squinted and focused, staring at the curtain, and startled herself when she could actually make something out—the shadowy outline of a figure that she assumed was standing just inside of the room.

Were they checking up on her? She hadn't heard the door open, or anyone enter.

Then it moved.

She drew in a sharp breath as she realised that whoever was in here with her had stepped forward, closer to the curtain.

Kirsty sat up in her bed, looking intently at the shadow, but couldn't see more than the vague shape of a person. The afforded light was simply not sharp enough. She listened, trying to make out the sound of breathing, but could hear none.

Was it a doctor, or nurse, coming in to check up on her? If so, why the stealth? She tried to keep herself calm, to stop her mind from running off to paranoid places, but could not. Panic began to rise, pushing up from her gut and into her chest, causing it to tighten.

'Hello?' she called out, her voice soft—almost trembling. There was no response. Kirsty also noticed that the shadow was eerily still, with no natural sway or movement to it.

Kirsty braced herself, expecting something to happen, but whoever it was remained motionless. They obviously knew Kirsty was aware of their presence, but had chosen not to reply. It almost felt like they were taunting her with their silence. She debated pulling back the curtain to reveal her mystery watcher, but the thought of doing so filled her with dread.

Get over it, Kirsty told herself. *You are safe here. You are in a hospital. There is no one here who is going to hurt you. There is an explanation for this. Stop being a coward and pull back the damn curtain.*

So she did.

Kirsty held out a shaking hand and took hold of the cotton material, grasping it firmly. Then, she braced herself and pulled. The curtain slid smoothly on its track and revealed the rest of the room behind.

There was no one there.

The light from the hallway seemed to blink back to its full level the moment the curtain was moved, and the coast was most certainly clear; given there were no nooks or crannies to this basic, square room, there was no place for anyone to hide.

And yet, Kirsty was certain she had seen someone—a shadow—inside of her room. She swung her legs from the bed, the wound on her back still stinging as she did, and got to her feet. She made her way to the door and looked out into the corridor beyond. It was a normal hospital hallway, with white walls, light blue linoleum flooring, and square panel lighting fixed into the ceiling tiles. No one was outside her room at present, but the general noise of the hospital—voices and the beeping of machines—could be heard in the distance. The lights outside flickered a little, even blinked out completely for a moment, but came back quickly.

Could that have been it? Simply a faulty light, creating the illusion of a shadow? Kirsty wasn't sure it explained things, as the outline she had seen seemed to be constant.

She did consider the fact that it could have all been in her head, given what she had been through, and the terrifying dream she just had. She supposed that was the most likely explanation for it—that there was never a shadow at all.

Kirsty moved back to her bed and sat down. She debated pulling the curtain back across, but felt safer with it open, as stupid as it sounded. She lay down on the bed again and got under the covers, wincing as a sharp pain radiated from the cuts on the small of her back. To ease the discomfort, she rolled to her side, facing the external wall—away from the light that spilt through from the door—and closed her eyes. Kirsty's mind bubbled with activity, and her heart rate was up, so she knew sleep could take a while. After a few minutes of slow breathing, Kirsty felt a familiar fatigue coming on again, creeping in around the edges. If she just tried to relax, then perhaps a good night's rest would eventually come. That proved to be the case, and she soon felt herself slipping away into a slumber... only for it to be yanked away as a sharp noise brought her back to full consciousness.

She knew instantly what that noise was—the sound of the curtain moving. Kirsty quickly rolled over in her bed to see that, yet again, the curtain had been pulled back across.

And the shadow had returned.

It was closer this time, and taller. She could make out more of its shape. Her breath caught in her chest as she saw a thin arm raise up and press an unnaturally long finger—or claw—up against the material of the curtain. The finger moved down, scraping its sharp edge against the cotton material.

Then Kirsty heard a strange noise—something she could not place. It sounded unnatural, inhuman. A kind of low, rumbling, growl, coming from whoever—or whatever—was behind the curtain.

She was about to scream for help when something else

caught her attention. Another sound, this one seeming very much human. It was a long, low moan, almost a wheeze, coming from somewhere very close.

Directly under the bed.

'Help,' Kirsty whimpered, her trembling voice barely above a whisper. Her body felt locked rigid with the terror that had overwhelmed her. Her mind was spinning, unable to comprehend what was happening.

What was that thing beyond the curtain? And who the hell was under her bed?

The moan from beneath her repeated itself, sounding pained, and continued for an exaggerated amount of time, keeping going long after it should have petered out. And then it changed, morphing into a strained, taunting chuckle. Kirsty heard some kind of shuffling on the floor, and then her heart froze at what she saw next.

Surely her eyes were tricking her?

A pale hand reached up and grabbed the metal frame of the bed.

The fingernails were black and the skin white, with splotches of yellows and purples. The thing behind the curtain continued to simply watch on as the person beneath the bed began to pull themselves up.

Kirsty saw the wet, stringy black hair first, as a head emerged from below the bed. Next, the top of a face pulled itself into view—milky eyes, wide and wild, with pupils that were dark, and red lines across the sclera in a distinct pattern... *what was that*? The shape of the lines was almost familiar, but Kirsty could focus on them no more as the full face then revealed itself to her, bearing a wide smile that showed blackened gums behind. Pronounced, dark veins crisscrossed the flesh of the strange woman, and an unnaturally long, black tongue snaked its way from a mouth that had curled into a snarl.

Kirsty heard that inhuman sound again, from the watcher beyond, as the woman—if that what she was—pulled herself up higher. Kirsty pushed herself to the far side of her bed and pulled her legs up to her chest, ready to release a scream of terror. The pale woman reached out a long arm as the clawing fingers came at Kirsty.

A scream erupted from Kirsty, and she shut her eyes and clamped her hands over her face, leaving enough space around her mouth for the sound of her desperate cries to escape. She yelled, over and over again—frantic, panicked, and absolutely hysterical. She braced herself, expecting the touch from that pale woman to come, one that she knew would be cold and clammy. The wait was as terrifying as the thought of that milky skin touching her own, and still, Kirsty continued to scream.

Then it came, the feeling she had been expecting. However, it was warmer than Kirsty had thought it would have been. She felt two hands take hold of her, by the shoulders, and begin to shake her. Through her own yelling, which now pained her throat, Kirsty heard a voice.

'What is it? Calm down, dear.'

The voice sounded warm and kind, even concerned. Kirsty opened her eyes and peeked through her fingers, and what she saw was not the ghostly, wild-eyed woman, but the round, reddened face of a nurse, wearing an expression of confusion.

Kirsty immediately looked past the nurse, and past the now-open curtain, looking for signs of the two strangers that had only moments earlier invaded her room.

There was no sign of them.

Kirsty quickly pulled herself away from the nurse and

leaned herself over the bed, hanging her head down to look beneath it. Yet again, the space was empty.

No, she thought to herself. *I couldn't have imagined that. It was too real. That couldn't have been in my head.*

'What is it, dear?' the nurse repeated, with a voice that matched her advanced years.

'I... I...' Kirsty started, but she didn't really know what to say. She continued to look frantically around the room, her head twisting this way and that. 'I thought I saw something.'

'What do you mean?' the nurse asked.

'Something in here. With me.'

The woman looked at her skeptically, and Kirsty knew instantly the nurse did not believe her. 'There is no one here, other than the two of us. I can promise you that, my dear.'

Kirsty made as if to argue, to insist that she was telling the truth, but stopped. Could she be certain of that? She knew what she *thought* she had seen, but she also knew that such things should not exist.

Through a mixture of fear, confusion, and pure exhaustion, Kirsty began to cry.

The nurse rested a comforting hand on Kirsty's shoulder. 'It's okay, you probably just had a bad dream or something. Nothing to be scared of.'

But Kirsty wasn't sure she believed that. And she spent the rest of the night wide awake, with the curtain pulled back. The light in the room remained switched on.

Morning's arrival seemed to take forever, with Kirsty constantly on edge, expecting the pale woman and the hidden watcher to once again return.

They didn't, not this night, but the morning was slow to arrive.

10

'So, what the hell happened?' Amanda asked, keeping her eyes on the road as she navigated the car from the hospital car park and out onto the adjoining main road.

Kirsty had been discharged shortly after her friend had arrived to pick her up, though the doctor who agreed to release her was worried about the 'episode' from last night, which Kirsty had persuaded him was due to stress and exhaustion. Thankfully, Amanda had not been privy to that conversation. Kirsty certainly didn't want the one person she trusted most doubting her sanity. Amanda's question was, in fact, referring to the attack.

'Just what I told you on the phone,' Kirsty replied. 'I got home on Friday night, went to bed, and woke up in the middle of the night. I thought I heard something on the stairs and poked my head out to look. Then I saw him, just standing there.'

Amanda gave a visible, almost exaggerated, shudder. 'That is creepy as hell,' she said.

'Yeah,' Kirsty agreed. 'And then he came at me. I managed to get by him and get downstairs, to the kitchen—'

'Why didn't you run outside?' Amanda asked, cutting her off.

'He'd locked the door,' Kirsty explained. 'But when I got into the kitchen I was trapped. He grabbed me and stuck me with this fucking needle, and it knocked me out. Then I woke up the next morning, with this... *mark*... carved into my back.'

'Jesus,' Amanda said, taking her hand from the car's gear stick and resting it on Kirsty's knee. She gave it a squeeze. 'Don't worry, I'll stay with you tonight. I've cancelled all my appointments for today and tomorrow.'

'You didn't have to—'

'It's non-negotiable, Kirsty,' Amanda interrupted. 'You don't need to worry about that.'

'Thanks,' Kirsty said, feeling incredibly grateful to her friend. The thought of eventually having to do that struck fear into her, and Kirsty knew she wouldn't sleep, constantly on edge, listening for the slightest sound and expecting someone to be in there with her. However, if Kirsty was completely honest with herself, she knew that after last night she was scared that there could be something else in the shadows as well... something much more unnatural, but no less evil.

The previous night's experience weighed heavily on her, and would not remove itself from her mind. Even when speaking with Amanda about her attack, the events of last night were always there--memories of that woman, pulling herself up from beneath the bed like a spectre dragging itself from the grave. And almost worse was that shadow— the watching figure—that loomed in the background.

Kirsty still couldn't decide if what she had seen was actually there, or if it had just been the result of a traumatised mind. On the one hand, the whole thing seemed so very real, but on the other… well, it was simply insanity to think such things could really exist. Kirsty had never been spiritual or believed in the supernatural, and secretly regarded those who did as either attention seekers, or misguided and confused souls.

So, what did that make her now?

The trip back to her home from the hospital was a relatively short one, and they arrived outside Kirsty's house a little over twenty minutes after setting off. Amanda pulled on the handbrake and turned to her friend. 'You ready?'

Kirsty wasn't sure she was. Going back into this house, her own home, was now an unsettling prospect, and Amanda seemed to sense that. The whole place now felt violated to Kirsty—no longer a home, now just a building where a horrible event had taken place.

It was a repeat of what had happened before, with Dom, in her last house. She had not been able to settle in that place, after Dom's actions, so would the same be true here? Would she now need to move again, uproot her entire life once more because of the actions of some fucking man?

She was torn. Both the idea of giving in to that, and also staying in this house, seemed equally unappealing to her. But she couldn't just sit in the car forever.

'I'm ready,' she told Amanda, and they both exited the car. Kirsty gazed out at her home. It looked like it always had, but it now felt different to her. A home that was no longer a home. She felt Amanda link an arm with hers, and the two walked inside together.

11

AMANDA AND KIRSTY spent the day inside, not setting foot out of the house. Amanda prepared them a dinner of oven-cooked fish and chips, given it was easy and quick to make, and was surprised to see how quickly Kirsty devoured her meal. They talked, but Kirsty seemed reluctant to go into much detail, especially about her stay at the hospital the previous night. Amanda didn't want to push what was clearly a raw, painful subject, but at the same time she didn't want her friend to fall into the same pit of self-loathing and isolation as she had after Dom. So, she poured them both a healthy glass of wine and, after the first drink, kept them flowing.

Before long, Amanda had her friend up on her feet, and was demonstrating the same self-defence manoeuvre she had tried to teach Kirsty a couple of nights ago. Of course, Kirsty had resisted, but Amanda thought a bit of light-hearted fun might help raise her spirits. Plus, Amanda hoped Kirsty would take something from it—get a taste for what she was capable of, just as Amanda had when Mike had first shown her.

Amanda really just hoped that Kirsty could see she didn't have to be the victim in life.

'Come on,' Amanda said, laughing, as they stood facing each other in the living room. 'I've shown you twice already. You can do this. Show me some aggression.' Amanda stepped forward, thrusting out her arm—which held a make-believe knife—and fully expected Kirsty to shy backward yet again. However, much to her surprise, her friend grabbed her wrist as shown, ducked, and twisted Amanda's arm around—but didn't quite have the strength to bend it in on itself and plunge the imaginary knife back into Amanda's chest.

'Damn it,' Kirsty said, stumbling a little. 'I almost had it.'

'You did,' Amanda agreed, 'just needed to believe a little more in what you were doing. Be more confident in yourself. Eye of the tiger and all that.'

'Well, I won't be picking up any boxing gloves anytime soon.'

'You don't need boxing gloves,' Amanda replied. 'A knee to the nuts would work better anyway.'

Kirsty swayed herself back to her large sofa before sinking down into it. She at least had a smile on her face. Amanda joined her on the sofa, plopping down next to her friend.

'So,' Amanda said. 'Honest answer. How are you feeling?'

Kirsty shook her head. 'I don't know. My head is still spinning. It all just seems like a dream, like it wasn't real. I suppose it probably wasn't.'

Amanda shook her head, more than a little confused. The first part made sense, but the second part certainly didn't. How could Kirsty think that what had happened to her hadn't been real?

'What do you mean, *probably wasn't real*?' Amanda asked, and Kirsty's eyes widened.

'I... I don't know,' Kirsty said with a slight stammer, but Amanda could see it was a lie. A cover. 'I'm just tired,' Kirsty went on. 'I meant to say it just feels like some kind of horrible dream.'

Kirsty then turned and looked to the corner of the room, away from Amanda, clearly not wanting to make eye contact.

'Kirsty,' Amanda said, setting a hand on her knee, 'what is it? What aren't you telling me? You can talk to me, hun, you know that.'

Kirsty paused, then slowly shook her head. 'You'll think I'm crazy.'

'How could you say that? Of course I won't. You know you can trust me.'

Yet again, Kirsty held back. Amanda could see there was something Kirsty was on the verge of saying, but was struggling to voice it. Amanda gave her time and, eventually, Kirsty spoke.

'You have to promise me you won't judge me. That you'll believe what I'm telling you.'

'Of course I'll believe you,' Amanda said, shocked that Kirsty would even doubt it.

Kirsty took a visible breath, as if what she was about to impart would be something monumental. Given what Amanda already knew, and how bad that had been, she had no idea what to expect.

'Last night, in the hospital... something happened,' Kirsty said.

'What?' Amanda asked, confused. What could possibly have happened in the security of a hospital? Had Kirsty had an episode, or had some seedy doctor or nurse tried something?

'I saw something, in my room,' Kirsty said. 'A figure, standing just behind the bed's curtain.'

'Someone was in your room, spying on you?' Amanda asked.

'I don't know. I pulled the curtain back, but no one was there,' Kirsty replied.

'Wait... so it was nothing? Like, just a shadow or something?'

'That's what I thought, so I ignored it and went back to sleep. But almost straight away I was woken up, and it was back. And it had moved.' Kirsty looked visibly shaken as she recounted the strange tale to Amanda. The blonde had an idea of the type of story this was turning into, one that would be difficult to believe, but Kirsty was not the type of girl to make up such things for sympathy.

Amanda listened as her friend went on. 'Then I heard something under the bed, and...' Kirsty's voice cracked, and she began to tear up. Even so, she pushed on. 'And a hand came up. I swear to God, Amanda, a fucking woman with dark hair pulled herself up from under my bed. She looked... wrong. I remember her reaching for me, then I lost it. I shut my eyes and started to scream.'

Amanda had no idea how to respond to what she'd just heard. She didn't want to dismiss what Kirsty was telling her, especially after seeing how upset it made her friend, but unless Amanda was mistaken, it seemed that Kirsty was describing an experience with the paranormal.

And that was just ridiculous.

'So what happened next?' Amanda asked, not really knowing what else to say. 'After she reached for you.'

'I don't know, really,' Kirsty said. 'I kept screaming, and

the next thing I know a nurse is there, asking me what's wrong.'

'And what happened to the woman?' Amanda asked.

'I don't know,' Kirsty repeated as she turned to face Amanda, looking more than a little embarrassed. A sad smile crossed her face. 'You don't believe me, do you?'

That was the issue: Amanda didn't believe her. She didn't believe that Kirsty had seen a woman pull herself up from beneath the hospital bed. However, she *did* believe that Kirsty *thought* she had seen something. Just that she was... confused.

'It's not that,' Amanda said. 'But let's look at this logically. You've just been through a fucking horrible experience. A fucking trauma. I'm willing to bet you were tired, too, right?'

Kirsty nodded. 'Yeah, exhausted.'

'Exactly. It could have just been some kind of dream, or a way for your mind to try to deal with the situation.'

'But it seemed so real,' Kirsty said. 'I know I wasn't dreaming. I was one hundred percent awake.'

'I believe you,' Amanda replied, 'but that doesn't mean it wasn't brought on by the shock of what happened. I mean come on, think about it, do you really believe you saw a ghost or something?'

Kirsty considered what her friend was saying, then shook her head. 'I suppose not.'

'Exactly.' Amanda put her arm around her friend and pulled her in for a hug. 'You don't need to feel ashamed or embarrassed. It's just a reaction to the attack, a way for your mind to try and process everything.'

'By showing me make-believe ghosts?'

'Well, I'm not a psychologist, hun. But I'm pretty certain you didn't actually see anything.'

Kirsty sighed. 'You're probably right. That's what I was trying to tell myself as well. It just seemed very real at the time. I thought, given how many people have probably died in that hospital, maybe even that room, that it could be, you know... haunted, or something. And I remember that horrible, decaying smell too.'

'Again,' Amanda said, 'all in your head.'

'I suppose,' Kirsty said, then pulled herself away from Amanda and looked her in the eye. She looked tired—absolutely worn out. 'So, you don't think I'm a nutcase?'

'No,' Amanda said, 'you definitely aren't a nutcase. You're a brave woman who has just been through something horrible. Give yourself a break.'

'I guess,' Kirsty said.

They spent the rest of the night chatting, and never returned to the topic of the supernatural or the undead. In truth, Amanda had been taken aback by Kirsty's outlandish story and had grown worried about her. She didn't believe that her friend was crazy, but at the same time it was concerning and was something Amanda knew she would have to keep an eye on. She didn't want Kirsty slipping into a bad place. Perhaps, after a good night's sleep, her friend would feel better. Amanda wasn't an expert in human psychology, and had no idea if what she was telling her friend—about it being the mind's way of dealing with things —had any merit. But it was better than letting Kirsty believe in the unbelievable.

They both went to bed early that night, and Amanda knew it would be a big test for her friend. She had suggested they both sleep downstairs, on the sofas, but Kirsty had said she needed to sleep in her own bed again. Amanda, therefore, took the spare room.

After using the toilet and brushing her teeth, Amanda

went into Kirsty's room to make sure her friend was comfortable. It didn't take long for Kirsty to drop off to sleep as exhaustion fully claimed her. Amanda pulled the sheets tight and left her friend to rest. She got into her own bed, hoping Kirsty would have a night of unbroken sleep, with no sign of any 'ghosts' or 'spirits' to further upset her.

Amanda was to be disappointed.

12

Kirsty opened her eyes to see darkness all around her. She was breathing heavily and sweating, her mind still reeling from the horrible nightmare that had just awakened her. Like the others, it had taken her to a place that her mind could only imagine was hell. There was no sign of Dom this time, only horrible things that had chased her and abused her beneath a swirling mass of alien stars. And, throughout it all, she had been watched by a shadowy figure that she could only make out in the edges of her peripheral vision.

She swallowed hard, her throat dry and, out of instinct, reached for her nightstand, where she normally kept a bottle of water. But tonight the stand was empty.

Damn it.

She steadied her breathing. *Just a dream, just a dream, just a dream.*

As much as she knew that to be true, Kirsty was surprised, and more than a little disappointed, at some of the horrible shit her mind was capable of coming up with.

After giving herself a moment, and checking the time—just after three in the morning—she pulled herself out of bed. She then, as quietly as possible, made for the door, desperate for both the toilet and for a drink of water. As Kirsty's hand reached for the handle, however, she paused, remembering the last time she'd opened the door in the middle of the night. Kirsty thought back to who had been waiting on the other side, standing on her stairs, hidden in shadows. Fear began to creep up from her gut, spidering its way through her body. But what else was she going to do? Wait in her bedroom until morning, like a child? She tried to push the fear back down, to control it—to own it—and then opened the door.

And there, in the darkness of the landing, was... absolutely nothing. All was as it should be. Kirsty could even hear the comforting sound of Amanda's heavy breathing from the next room, reminding her that she wasn't alone. She crept along the landing and into the bathroom, gently closing the door behind her and turning on the light.

After relieving herself, Kirsty washed her hands and kept the cold water running from the faucet. She ducked her head down and began to pull in long gulps from the stream of cool liquid, wetting her dry throat. The water felt good, and she kept gulping down more and more, only stopping when her stomach lurched. She stood up straight once more, turned off the tap, and wiped her mouth on the towel. She then turned... and stopped.

The door to the bathroom was wide open.

Kirsty had, without question, closed it behind her.

The familiar feeling of fear re-introduced itself, something that was becoming far too familiar to Kirsty, and far too unwelcome. Looking out into the dark landing beyond, Kirsty could see no one. She tried to think rationally, as Amanda would want her to; what were the chances the same man had broken into her house again to have his way with her? Hadn't he done everything he wanted to last time? Her mind then leapt back to the hospital, to the woman, and to the shadowy figure. The panic began to build.

No!

Kirsty admonished herself. There were no such things as ghosts, and she needed to stop being scared of shadows. She wouldn't allow her mind to run away with itself again. After taking a steadying breath, she forced her mind to work everything through.

She had closed the door after she'd entered the bathroom, that she was sure of, but she had not locked it. Perhaps it just wasn't fully closed and had simply drifted open of its own accord. The door was a good quality one, solid with an expensive oak veneer, and had never taken to drifting open on its own before now. Then again, doors could drop in their hinges after a few years of use. Maybe it just needed re-aligning?

That certainly seemed plausible. Much more so than fucking ghosts following her back from the hospital. It was also more likely than her attacker returning for seconds.

Wasn't it?

He'd had every chance to finish what he needed to after Kirsty had been drugged—a thought that sickened her beyond words—so why would he need to return and risk getting caught or recognised? Then again, a man who was willing to drug a woman and carve some weird symbol into her skin was not exactly going to be thinking rationally. Perhaps he needed to come back to finish whatever he had set in motion a few nights ago? Maybe it was a two-stage deal, some horrible satanic thing that he needed to complete.

Kirsty shook her head, realising that despite her best efforts, her mind had indeed run away with itself again. And she hated it. Was this to be her life now? One of living in constant fear of what lurked in the shadows?

After a few more moments of standing motionless in the bathroom, waiting for something to happen, Kirsty eventually plucked up the courage to leave. She stepped out onto the landing and peeked down the stairs.

All clear.

She listened carefully, trying to make out footsteps of any kind from elsewhere in the house. But the only thing she could hear was the sound of Amanda's breathing. Angry with herself for getting so worked up over nothing, Kirsty switched off the bathroom light and made her way back to her bedroom.

Once into bed, she lay down, listening to the silence of the night, and again told herself there was nothing to be afraid of.

Kirsty closed her eyes in an effort to relax her body and help reclaim sleep. No sooner than she had shut them, however, her eyes snapped open again upon hearing what sounded like a sharp intake of breath in the room.

Her head snapped to her side, towards the direction of the noise and the far corner of her room—one that swam in shadows and pure darkness. She squinted, trying to peer through the black, but was unable to penetrate it. Normally, the low light generated by the moonlight outside would have been enough to cut through the darkness, but at the moment that was not so. The dark that completely enveloped the corner seemed abnormal and absolute. Kirsty then heard a different sound, but one that was hauntingly familiar. She drew in a breath. It was the same unnatural growl that she had heard in the hospital the previous night. The one from the shadow behind the curtain, the same one that she was now certain stood in the corner of her room, hidden within a sea of black.

The growl rumbled again, louder this time, and Kirsty sat up in her bed, suddenly aware of what that noise had previously brought forward. Was that horrible spectre of a woman once again lying below Kirsty? Was she just beneath Kirsty's bed, about to pull herself up into view?

Kirsty shot out her hand and hit the touch-lamp that sat on her night-stand. It snapped on and lit up, and two more quick taps increased the brightness to its maximum level. The light pushed its way out, finally breaking down the dark corner where the unknown thing seemed to be hiding. However, the light did not reveal the mysterious watcher, only the empty corner of Kirsty's room—a completely normal space where the two white walls ran into each other.

Kirsty let out a breath she had been holding, relieved that there was nothing there, but also certain that the sound had not been in her head. It wasn't a dream or trick of the mind.

It was real.

And yet... she could see for herself—now that the shadows had been pushed away by the light—that there was nothing there.

Kirsty let her head drop back to rest on the pillow, feeling frustration and anger grow.

Then, the bedside light blinked out, and Kirsty was again plunged into darkness.

She sat back up in bed and heard that low, taunting growl again. Not knowing what else to do, Kirsty readied herself to scream, hoping to alert Amanda. Perhaps her friend's presence alone would be enough to banish this thing, as had happened with the nurse showing up the previous night. But, before she was able to yell out, Kirsty became aware of an intense feeling of cold emanate from her right. And there was something else, too: a presence, one that she could detect looming over her.

She braced herself, fearful of what she would see, and turned her head.

As it turned out, her fears were well-founded. Kirsty had expected to see that same ghostly woman from the hospital, but what she actually saw was someone else: a tall man, with pale skin that was laced with deep purple veins. He was completely naked, and his short, stubby penis flopped close to Kirsty's head. However, her focus was further up, on his face, as she looked at his milky eyes and dull pupils. In the sclera, Kirsty saw red lines in a pattern, just like she had seen on the woman who had pulled herself up from the bed in the hospital. But at this distance, she was able to make out the detail more clearly, and she could see that etched into the flesh of his eyes was the very same mark that had been carved into her lower back.

The man's mouth and black lips pulled into a smile, revealing crooked and pointy teeth. A rotting smell, like sour milk, washed over Kirsty.

All of these details were noticed in an instant—in the short time it took for her to breathe in and push out a terrified scream as loudly as she could.

She felt a cold hand grab her shoulder as the gangly figure gripped her tightly, closer to her now, bent at the waist. Panic rose, freezing Kirsty in place, leaving her capable of only screaming and yelling. The smell grew worse as the nightmarish thing lowered its head towards her.

Then the light to the room came on.

Kirsty, still screaming, spun her head to see the door

swing open and Amanda step into view, fists clenched, braced for action, with a panicked look on her face.

'What's wrong?' Amanda asked, her breathing rapid.

How can she ask what's wrong? Kirsty thought. *Surely she can see...*

But when Kirsty turned back, the man was gone. And the previously dark corner was now fully illuminated from the main bedroom light above.

Amanda went straight over to her, sitting on the bed, grabbing Kirsty gently by the arms. 'What happened?' she asked, eyes wide.

Kirsty was unable to formulate the words at first. She knew, beyond any doubt, that whatever was happening had not just been in her head. Whether she could fully explain it or not, Kirsty was now certain that it was very real.

'I... I saw something again,' Kirsty eventually said between sobbing breaths. 'I swear, Amanda, I saw something.'

Amanda's head quickly swivelled around the room. 'What?' she asked, concerned.

Kirsty cast a quick glance down to her shoulder, still feeling the after-effects of that cold grip, and saw the faint outline of fingerprints. 'I... I don't know,' she said. 'A man, standing above my bed.'

That familiar look of doubt crossed Amanda's face, the same one Kirsty had seen earlier, and it made Kirsty feel upset. She hated the fact her friend didn't believe her, but she knew for certain now that whatever this was, it wasn't just her imagination.

'Hun,' Amanda said as if comforting a child. 'You need to calm down. There is no-one here. Perhaps it was just—'

'It wasn't a fucking dream!' Kirsty snapped. She was tired of everything right now. Tired of being scared, tired of the exhaustion, tired of feeling crazy, and tired of not being believed. 'I'm telling you, what I saw was real.'

Amanda just hugged her, pulling Kirsty's head down to her chest. 'It's going to be okay,' she said.

Kirsty wasn't sure she believed that and felt like she was losing her mind. These visions, or experiences, seemed to have started the night after the attack, the night everything changed for her. When that fucking mark had been cut into her—the same one she had just seen on the ghostly man's eyeball—concentric circles with an inverted triangle inside. There had to be a link. It seemed insane to think it, but what else made sense?

Kirsty continued to sob as Amanda tried to console her.

What would happen if this never ended? If she kept seeing these terrifying things for the rest of her life? Or worse, what if the things that seemed to be stalking her were not satisfied to just follow and had intentions that were much more insidious?

The two didn't speak again that night, and at some point, they fell asleep in the bed together, still embraced, with Kirsty finally getting some uneasy rest.

The whole time, they were both watched by something beyond their understanding.

Something that had designs on Kirsty's very soul.

13

THE SMELL of the eggs frying in the pan only served to make Amanda's stomach growl and rumble. She was equal parts ravenous, tired, and grumpy, following an uncomfortable night's sleep that amounted to only a few hours. She hoped the eggs that Kirsty had insisted she prepare—while Amanda served up the coffee—would go some way to making her feel better.

Things between the two of them had been a little off since last night. Not quite strained, but certainly not right. And Amanda knew why: Kirsty was upset that Amanda didn't fully believe her account of what happened. And while Amanda didn't doubt Kirsty *thought* she had seen something, she wanted her friend to realise what was really going on; and yet the two of them hadn't been able to resolve that in the few hours since they'd woken up.

Kirsty had already called her workplace to advise them of what had happened, and that she would need a few days off, if that was okay. Amanda had winced at that.

Don't ask if it's okay, demand it.

After what had happened, Kirsty had no reason to tiptoe around what she needed and was entitled to. While the telephone conversation seemed an awkward one—at least as far as Amanda could tell—Kirsty's employer seemed understanding and granted her time off, and just asked that Kirsty keep them informed on when she would be returning to work.

Amanda had also cleared her schedule today, pushing her clients back to a date later in the week. That meant that things would be hectic when she got back into it, as she tried to play catch-up with her personal training sessions, but that didn't matter to her—she was doing what she felt she should and helping a friend.

The sound of the eggs cooking in the pan was a welcome one—a hint of normality that would hopefully take their minds off things. The glorious morning outside helped, too, as the sun streamed in through the windows, into the open-floorplan kitchen. Had the shadow of the last few days not been hanging over them, it could have been an idyllic morning for the pair.

Kirsty began to serve up the food, placing the eggs on two plates, next to the rashers of crispy bacon that she had prepared a few minutes before. She approached the break-fast bar and set down both plates, and Amanda added salt and pepper to her dish, letting Kirsty do the same before they both dug in. The eggs were thick and runny, and the bacon salty and crunchy—absolutely delicious. She took two more greedy mouthfuls before pulling in a long sip of her steaming coffee. It tasted good and warmed her stomach.

Amanda knew she would soon have to speak to Kirsty to put things right—after all, she was here to help her friend through a difficult time—but felt that conversation would flow much better if they were both operating on full stomachs and injections of caffeine.

Once their plates were clean, Amanda set about building bridges. 'Look,' she started. 'I don't want you to feel like you can't trust me, or that I don't believe you, it's just that I—'

She was cut off by the ringing of Kirsty's mobile phone. Kirsty looked at the screen and wrinkled her nose, clearly not recognising the number.

'Should I ignore it?' she asked, and Amanda shrugged. 'Fuck it,' Kirsty said. She hit answer and brought the phone up to her ear. 'Hello?' She paused as the other person spoke, and her eyes opened a little wider. She then covered the microphone with her hand and turned to Amanda. 'It's the detective who is looking after my case,' she whispered.

Perhaps they had caught the guy? Amanda prayed that was the case, and hoped it would help Kirsty. Knowing that the man who had attacked her would be locked up and punished for what he'd done would surely help put Kirsty's mind to rest.

And that fucker had a lot to be punished for.

'HELLO, DETECTIVE,' Kirsty said, feeling apprehensive after the man on the other end of the phone had introduced himself as DC Phillips. He had spoken in a deep, aged voice. 'Do you have any news?' she asked, praying that he did.

Kirsty had previously been told that the case would be given to a Detective Constable to handle, and he would soon be in touch—it seemed now was that time.

Kirsty had presumed that he would have come around to

see her in person, rather than making a phone call, but she guessed it was what it was. And, if he was calling with good news—like the apprehension of the bastard who'd broken into her home—she was more than happy with a phone call. Kirsty briefly wondered if she would get to speak to the man who had attacked her. It was doubtful, but part of her wanted that to happen as she really wanted to ask him a few questions.

The first being: why her?

And the second: what was the mark, and was it responsible for the things she'd been seeing?

Lastly: how can she make it stop?

It turned out that none of those questions were close to being answered as yet, and DC Phillips gave her a disappointing update.

'I just wanted to call and touch base with you,' he said.

'Okay,' Kirsty replied. 'Did you find him?'

'No, not as of yet,' DC Phillips replied. 'I really just wanted to introduce myself to you, so you know who I am, and so you know who you should contact if you need anything.'

'Ah, okay,' Kirsty said, not bothering to hide the disappointment in her voice. 'Any leads?'

'Well,' he said, sounding uncomfortable—a clear sign that he had none, 'we conducted a thorough investigation of your home, but found very little. A few fibres from his clothing, which isn't much to go on, really. The examination on you at the hospital also turned up very little.'

It could have just been Kirsty misreading his tone, but that comment almost sounded accusatory—as if he were blaming her and her body for not providing more information.

'And what about him cutting me?' she asked.

'I don't follow,' he replied.

'What does it mean? The mark?'

'In what regard?'

Kirsty was initially lost for words. Was the man tasked with cracking the case really so dense?

'In the regard that it is a weird fucking symbol that he cut into my skin. What does it mean? Does it have any significance?'

'Oh,' he said dismissively. There was even a slight trace of a chuckle in his voice. 'Don't worry about that, I don't think it means much. It's likely he was either high or mentally unstable. Chances are he had seen that symbol somewhere and thought he would have a go at recreating it.'

Kirsty exploded. 'You guess? You fucking guess?! How about you stop fucking guessing and take this seriously. Have you even looked into what that mark could mean? Has this kind of thing been done to anyone else? Why are you just dismissing it?'

'Ma'am, please calm down,' he replied, which didn't calm her at all—his condescending tone only enraged her further. 'I have looked into similar incidents we have on file recently, but none have any kind of mark or symbol cut into the victim. Most incidents of this kind are spur of the moment, where an attacker sees an opportunity. That, or the attacker knows the victim. So, we are looking into all CCTV in the area that we can find, and also we will need to come over to speak to you again, to see if you can think of anyone who would want to do this to you.'

'No one I know would do this,' she snapped.

'Okay,' he said, actually having the nerve to sound exacerbated with her. 'I'm not trying to upset you, Mrs. Thompson—'

'Miss Thompson!' Kirsty cut in. 'For the love of God! Do you even know what you are doing?'

'Please, *Miss* Thompson, just remain calm. I don't want to upset you any further, and I'm sorry if I have,' he said, sounding anything but sincere. 'Are you available today? I will come by as soon as I can, if that's okay. We can talk then.'

Kirsty sighed. 'Fine. I'll be in.'

'Okay, I'll give you a full update when I'm there, and ask any questions I need to. Thank you for your time.'

The detective didn't even give Kirsty a chance to say anything else, not even a goodbye, and ended the call.

'That cheeky motherfucker!' Kirsty yelled, seething. She looked over to her friend and saw that Amanda's jaw was hanging open.

'That didn't seem to go well,' she said.

'No, it didn't,' Kirsty replied, throwing her hands up in the air. 'It sounds as if the police have given me Inspector—fucking—Clouseau to solve the case.'

Amanda let out a quick snort.

'It's not funny,' Kirsty shot back. But, even as she did, she felt herself laugh a little as well.

'I know it isn't,' Amanda said. 'But you know what, it's good to see you angry.'

'What do you mean?'

'Exactly what I say. You've been nothing but scared these last few days. It's good to see you stand up for yourself and let your anger show. You have a lot to be angry about, Kirsty. And if you're angry, then that means you are fighting. And I'd much rather that than see you too scared to sleep.'

Kirsty considered her friend's words and realised she had a point. At that very moment, Kirsty didn't feel scared at all, only a mixture of anger and, in a weird way, relief. Like her explosion at 'Inspector Clouseau' had released some of the pressure that had been building within.

And it felt good.

However, beneath all that, there was still the lingering notion that nagged at Kirsty and would not let go; she couldn't help but think that the symbol on her back and the recent weird occurrences were all connected.

And she could feel that things were somehow about to get worse.

14

GIVEN there might not be a lot of time before the detective was due to show up, Kirsty and Amanda decided that they both needed to ready themselves and freshen up. With only one bathroom, Kirsty insisted that Amanda go shower first. It would be quicker for her, as Kirsty had to check her wound, then re-dress it as the nurses had shown her. Something she was not looking forward to.

But that was not Kirsty's sole reason for suggesting her friend use the bathroom first.

Amanda had done as requested and gone up to shower, leaving Kirsty in the kitchen. Once she was alone, Kirsty quickly retrieved her laptop and set it on the breakfast bar. She didn't know how much time she had to work with, but knew that Amanda would not be pleased if she caught Kirsty obsessing over the symbol on her body, as Kirsty planned to find out exactly what it meant.

As the laptop was powering up, she took off her t-shirt and started to gingerly pull away the dressing that was taped to her back and covering the wound. It stung, and the tape left black marks on her skin as it came away. Soon the top half was pulled free, and the dressing hung down, exposing the wound below. Kirsty twisted, trying to look down to see the horrible marking—two circles, with an inverted triangle in their centre—but at this angle it was impossible to get a clear view. She had only seen the cuts once before—in her living room mirror, just after the police officers had arrived on the scene—but for what she wanted to try, she would need to see it in much more detail.

She grabbed her phone and snapped a few pictures as best she could, hoping one would show it clearly enough. She quickly flicked through the images and paused on the one that was most clear. Not a perfect shot by any stretch, but enough to give clarity.

The sight of her skin, defiled in such a way, made Kirsty's stomach drop. Would the mark heal completely, or scar this way, forever branding her? The nurse who dressed it had said there was a possibility of scarring, but plastic surgery was an option to help remove it. Kirsty didn't want that, didn't want any of it—she just wanted it gone. Because if it was gone, wouldn't that mean those... *things*... following her around would then leave her alone?

She studied the picture she had taken.

The mark on her reddened skin was both crude yet intricate; the lines were not as straight and clean as they looked like they should have been, yet the symbol was clear and unmistakable. It was comprised of two concentric circles, one outside of the other and about an inch apart. The inner circle was about six inches in diameter, and between these two circles were odd markings, very basic in design—a short wavy line, an X, and two perpendicular lines, amongst others. Lastly, and perhaps most strikingly, was an inverted triangle that sat centrally within the inner ring, pointing down, each tip connecting with the inside of the circle. A line ran from the top to the bottom tip of the triangle, separating it into two equal sides.

To say that it looked occult-like, or satanic, was an understatement.

Kirsty emailed the picture to herself, and then opened it up on her laptop, viewing it on a larger screen. Up above, she heard the shower start in the bathroom.

The enlarged image showed things in more horrible detail, but revealed little else in terms of information for Kirsty to go on. So, she then opened up her web browser, moved to a search engine, and typed in *symbol, two circles, inverted triangle.*

It brought up some options. Kirsty clicked on the images tab, which accompanied the search results, then scanned what was shown, to see if there were any matches. While some were close, none of them looked to be the same symbol. Not exactly.

She continued to flick through the list and tried refining her search a little, but again came up short. Worse, she knew Amanda would soon be finished and would come down. If she caught Kirsty in what she was doing, then Amanda would no doubt make her stop... or try to.

What else can I try?

Not that Kirsty had tried much as yet, in all honesty, having been stumped after one quick Google search. Was that the extent of an investigation for the people of today? She had visions of her own detective—the inept Clouseau—typing away on at his desk, using a search engine, then throwing up his hands in defeat.

Can't find anything on Google, he'd say. *This case is unsolvable.*

But Kirsty was not about to give up. Just because Google didn't have the answer didn't mean the wider internet didn't.

She then opened up a discussion website she frequented, called Reddit. Kirsty had joined the site a little while ago, and it was one filled with message boards on pretty much every subject matter under the sun. After carrying out a quick subreddit search, using the word *occult,* Kirsty was pleased to see multiple results. She chose the most popular one and had a quick look through both the *hot* and *new* topics. It was clear that most people on the forum strongly believed in what they were talking about—occultism, conspiracy theories, black magic—and more than a few posts were centred on the discussion of certain symbols. Perhaps there was someone lurking on the board who could help.

It might have been a stupid thing to do, but Kirsty felt she had little choice. Amanda had said she should show more fight, and that was what she planned to do. Kirsty didn't want to sit around and wait for things to happen—she wanted to be pro-active, to try and get to the bottom of it herself.

She then heard the steady hum of the shower above shut off, indicating Amanda had finished. It wouldn't be long now until her friend came back down, and Kirsty needed to be finished before then. She quickly made a post, asking for help:

This might not be the normal thing you find here, but please believe me. I was attacked a few nights ago in my home. The man who attacked me has not been caught. While I was unconscious, he cut a symbol into my lower back, and I'm desperate to find out what it means. If anyone can help, I would really appreciate it.

After reading it, Kirsty considered revising the plea, changing it to make it sound less desperate, but she knew that she didn't have the time. The important thing was to put the picture up and see if anyone could help.

She uploaded the photo, took a breath, and hit the *submit* button. The page refreshed, and she saw that her post, which was titled, *What is this symbol?* was at the top. Hopefully, it would yield some results.

Kirsty quickly powered down the laptop and put it away before haphazardly re-applying the dressing to the wound on her back and pushing the tape down onto her skin. Much of it did not stick, but it would be enough until she could re-dress it herself after her shower.

Given that Kirsty had the Reddit app on her mobile phone, she was tempted to check it already to see if there had been any replies, but knew that she needed to give it a little time.

She then began to pace around the kitchen, aware that a nervous energy was starting to rise inside of her. Now that she had done what she'd needed to, Kirsty felt jittery and impatient.

As she paced and passed the doorway to the kitchen that looked out into the main hallway, Kirsty paused. Something had caught her attention—a quick movement on the stairs. It was all too brief, disappearing up out of view almost as quickly as she had seen it. As if something had moved upstairs.

There was no sound, however, and no creaking of the stair boards. Kirsty then slowly made her way to the bottom of the stairs and looked up.

Nothing.

She could see the door to the bathroom was still closed, which meant Amanda was inside. But there was no movement out here.

As much as she was not about to doubt herself after recent events, perhaps this time it truly had been nothing.

She turned to move back into the kitchen, and then heard a thud from upstairs.

Had Amanda fallen? Kirsty ran back to the bottom of the stairs and again looked up to the bathroom door. She could detect other noises now, as if something were rolling about on the bathroom floor.

The sound of a struggle.

She then heard Amanda scream.

15

AMANDA LEFT KIRSTY DOWNSTAIRS, at her own request, to go shower and change for the day. Amanda had brought a change of clothes with her, as well as her toiletries, knowing that she would be spending some time at Kirsty's to help see her through the next few days. After receiving that initial horrible phone call from her friend, Amanda herself had been filled with panic and anger.

The thought of that man—*no, not a man, that fucking weasel*—running around free out there after doing what he'd done, with the potential to do it to others, stirred up a familiar resentment against the unfairness of it all. It was the same feeling Amanda had gotten when she'd found out Dom would be getting away with his attack.

And, given the way the phone call with the detective had gone, Amanda didn't hold much hope in the police catching their man.

The thoughts played on her mind as Amanda readied herself for her shower—setting the nozzle to full and turning up the heat. She stepped inside, feeling the water that was not quite scalding, but wasn't far off, blast against her skin, helping to wash away the last of the grogginess that the breakfast and coffee hadn't quite overcome.

The room quickly steamed up as the extract fan hummed and worked hard, given little chance to combat the humidity that was rapidly building and making the modestly sized bathroom resemble a steam room. Perhaps not the best shower etiquette in someone else's house, but Amanda knew that Kirsty would not mind. Amanda enjoyed her showers like this—hot and strong—to help her detox and unwind. There was a lot on her mind at the moment, so she savoured the chance to let it all drift away, if only for a short time.

After standing for a few minutes and just enjoying the feeling of the hot, powerful stream of water pepper her skin, Amanda began to soap herself up. Looking beyond the glass shower-screen that was fixed to the side of the bath, it was a struggle to actually make out the opposite wall, such was the thickness of the swirling mist in the room.

Maybe I'm overdoing it, Amanda thought, deciding that perhaps it would be best to crack a window. Before she did, however, she paused and squinted.

Was that just a trick of the light?

In the far corner of the room, near the sink, there seemed to be a dark mass behind the thick moisture that clouded the air. The black shape took on a human-like form and, confused, Amanda brought up her hand and wiped it down the glass screen, clearing some of the water away and allowing for a clearer view. She squinted, but the outline she thought she had seen seemed to dissolve as the steam moved and swirled. She shook her head.

You're getting worse than Kirsty.

Amanda knew that what she had seen was a kind of faces-in-the-fire effect, where the brain makes sense of random patterns by associating it with shapes that it recognises, but aren't actually representative of what it is seeing.

She confirmed to herself that that was what it must have been, and nothing more.

Amanda moved her way to the far side of the bath, feeling the water slosh around her feet. A window with frosted glass sat on the external wall, and Amanda pulled at the handle and eased it open, allowing some of the mist to escape the room. The breeze from outside felt a little cold against her skin, so she quickly moved back under the stream of hot water to rinse off. As she was wiping the suds from her body, Amanda turned her head to the side, again looking through the shower screen. The steam in the room had dissipated somewhat, allowing her to see a little more clearly.

There was no dark shadow standing in the corner.

In that moment, Amanda did feel for Kirsty. After going through what she had, not only with her attacker but also with Dom, it was only natural for Kirsty to be more easily spooked. Was it any wonder that Kirsty was having these 'experiences'? Hell, Kirsty's insistence that she had been seeing things had caused Amanda to question herself, momentarily though it was.

Another blast of cold air hit Amanda from behind. Not quite a breeze, just an intense radiating chill that enveloped her. Goosebumps formed on her skin, which started to ruin the shower. Amanda figured she'd aired out the room enough now, so she decided to shut the window and enjoy a few more minutes under the hot, blasting water. However, before she turned to do so, the cold increased, and she felt an icy touch on her back.

Amanda let out a gasp and spun around. She half-expected to see something behind her, standing in the shower with her... but there was nothing. As she did turn, however, for the briefest of moments, Amanda again thought she saw that dark shadow, this time standing just beyond the shower screen, blurred by the running water. But when she concentrated, she could see nothing.

Damn it, girl. Get your head together.

She shut the window and quickly jumped back beneath the flowing water, now feeling a little unnerved and eager to finish up and get back downstairs. She shouldn't be feeling like this and was annoyed at herself for getting so anxious. Amanda let the hot water wash away the feeling of cold that seemed to permeate into her bones—something that took longer than she thought it should have, considering the heat pouring down from the shower-head—and, once done, shut off the shower and pushed open the screen. She grabbed one of the folded towels she had set on the closed toilet lid and began to dry off, still standing in the bath as she did.

Once dry enough, she stepped out and onto the tiled floor, wrapping the towel around herself. She used another to dry off the rest of her body where needed, including her face. However, almost as soon as the cotton material covered her face, another feeling of intense cold washed over her, and the towel suddenly snapped tighter around her head. Startled, Amanda gripped the cloth and yanked, trying to rip it away from her face... but it would not budge. She felt the material wrap tighter and pull back, as if someone were trying to suffocate her with it.

It made no sense. She was alone in that room.

What the fuck was going on?

Amanda reached an arm back, but felt nothing behind her, yet still, the towel was being pulled hard, yanking her head back, smothering her mouth. She began to flail, twisting her body this way and that, kicking out behind her into empty air.

No, no, no. This can't be happening.

As she squirmed, Amanda felt her feet slip out beneath her, and she fell to the floor. The pressure of the material around her face remained constant, however. She quickly twisted her body again, so that she was face down, and thankfully felt the towel give a little.

It had to have been her imagination—her panicked mind running away with itself—but from beneath the hood that blocked out her vision, Amanda was certain she could hear a low groan, one that turned into a definite, mocking chuckle. The vile sound was quiet, as if meant only for her.

Then the towel fell slack. She was able to quickly pull it free and throw it to the floor.

Amanda pushed herself upright and slid back, kicking out at the damp towel in order to get it away from her as she wheezed and panted, trying to suck clean air into her body —which was difficult given the moisture that drifted about all around her. Amanda's eyes darted around the room, but there was no one else there. Absolutely nothing to see.

Once she had enough air in her body, Amanda let out a scream.

16

Kirsty took the stairs two at a time, reaching the top in a flash.

She tried the bathroom door and, thankfully, found it open. Bursting into the room, she peered through the fogged-up space to see Amanda on the floor, back pressed against the toilet, looking horrified. The girl had a towel wrapped around herself, and another lay discarded on the floor in a small heap.

'What happened?' Kirsty asked as she rushed over to her friend. She took hold of the shaking girl and felt her trembling in her hands. Amanda's eyes were wide with fear, but she just shook her head. 'What is it?' Kirsty pressed. An awful feeling started to knot itself up in Kirsty's gut—the way Amanda looked now, shaking and terrified, was probably the same way Kirsty had looked the previous night when Amanda had burst in on her.

Had she experienced something too?

The thought was unnerving, as it would confirm that what had been happening was real. But, at the same time—and as ashamed as Kirsty was for even thinking it—there was a sense of relief in that. It would mean that she wasn't going crazy, at least.

'What did you see?' Kirsty asked, but Amanda wouldn't talk at first. Eventually, however, she did seem to calm down a little. The shaking stopped and her quick breathing slowed.

'I don't know what happened,' Amanda eventually said, and Kirsty recognised a look of embarrassment wash over her friend. 'It was stupid.'

'What do you mean?' Kirsty asked. 'What was stupid?'

'Nothing,' Amanda replied. 'I got the towel tangled around my face and panicked. Then I fell.'

'Are you sure?' Kirsty asked confused, and a little disappointed. 'The way you screamed... I don't know, it just sounded like something had scared you.'

Amanda shook her head, and then got to her feet. Her legs shook a little as she stood, but she managed to keep her footing. 'No, I just scared myself over nothing, really. Like I said, it was stupid. Sorry for scaring you.'

Kirsty got up as well, not certain if Amanda was holding back on her, or if what her friend was saying was actually true—meaning she hadn't seen anything, and Kirsty was still alone in all of this. Another pang of guilt sprang up from her gut as she realised how disappointing that thought was to her. Why was she so eager for her closest friend to suffer the same experiences?

Well, that was an easy question to answer. Selfish as it may have been, it would mean that Kirsty wasn't crazy. And, after all, misery loves company. It would confirm that Kirsty's experiences were real, and somehow validate the fear she was feeling.

'I'll be fine,' Amanda said. 'Honestly.'

Kirsty wanted to push things further. She knew Amanda

well and could tell her friend was hiding something, but Kirsty did not get the chance. The sound of the doorbell ringing out startled them both.

'Looks like Inspector Clouseau is here,' Amanda said. 'You go and speak to him. I'll get myself ready and be down as quickly as I can.'

Amanda didn't wait for Kirsty to agree and instead walked past her and disappeared into the bedroom she was staying in, closing the door behind her.

Kirsty let out a sigh as she hadn't even had time to shower yet. She quickly jogged into the bedroom and looked herself over in the mirror, making sure she was at least presentable. Her hair was up in a ponytail, and she wore baggy jogging bottoms and a wrinkled white t-shirt, but she was passable. Well, she would have been if she hadn't looked so damn tired. Heavy, purple bags hung under her eyes, and she actually appeared a little gaunt. Whether or not that was possible after only a few days of her mental torment, she didn't know, but that was how it looked to her.

The doorbell rang again. Kirsty swore to herself, annoyed at the visitor's impatience, and ran downstairs. When she pulled open the door, she knew immediately that the short, scruffy man who stood outside was indeed Detective Constable Phillips.

The man was a walking cliché, actually wearing a faded grey trench coat and an equally worn wide-brimmed fedora to match. His coat was open, allowing Kirsty to see a white, creased shirt with one side untucked. He had a few days' worth of grey stubble on a stony face that was well-weathered. The man took off his hat to reveal a mess of ashy hair.

'Miss Thompson?' he asked, and Kirsty recognised his gravelly voice from the phone call earlier.

'Yes,' Kirsty confirmed. 'I take it you're DC Phillips?'

The man nodded. 'That's right.' He then pulled out his identification and showed it to Kirsty. She had no idea what to look out for on such things, having never seen police identification before, but thought it looked authentic enough. The man then put it back into his pocket and waited to be invited inside, fidgeting with his hat and rotating it in stubby fingers that had nails chewed down to the wick.

Kirsty stepped back and pulled the door open wider. 'Come in.'

'Thank you,' he replied and stepped inside, allowing Kirsty to close the door before leading the way. Kirsty took him through to the kitchen and motioned to the breakfast bar. 'Take a seat.'

'Thank you,' DC Phillips replied and hopped up onto one of the stools. 'Someone upstairs?' he asked.

Kirsty realised he was referring to the footsteps, slight as they were, that Amanda was making while getting herself ready.

'Yes, my friend stayed here last night. Didn't want me being on my own, you know?'

Phillips nodded and set his hat down on the breakfast bar counter top.

'Can I take your coat?' Kirsty asked.

'No, it's fine.'

'How about a coffee? A drink of any kind?'

He shook his head. 'No, thank you.'

'Okay,' Kirsty said, feeling every bit of awkwardness the exchange brought up. She always thought that police officers, especially detectives, would need some semblance of people skills. But she should have known from their phone call earlier that the man would be severely lacking in that regard.

She took a seat opposite him. 'You got here pretty quick,' she told him.

'I managed to get clear of what I was doing,' he replied, 'so managed to fit in the trip over here straight away.' He made it sound like this whole trip was an inconvenience that he could do without.

You and me both, buddy.

'Okay,' Kirsty said, just wanting to get on with things. 'So, what have you found out?'

He shrugged. 'Not a great deal, I'm afraid. Like I said on the phone earlier, we didn't get much from our search of your home, or the results of your examination. We're still looking into the CCTV in the area, but we haven't found anything as yet.'

'You said before that this kind of thing is usually either people who have spotted an opportunity, or likely be someone who knows me?'

'That's right,' Phillips said.

'Don't you think it's weird that we have nothing to go on? If this was someone who just saw an opening, or someone I knew, then that doesn't strike me as the kind of person who would leave no evidence behind. Whoever this was, they obviously knew what they were doing.'

'Well, let's not leap to any conclusions.'

'It isn't a leap,' Kirsty insisted. 'Your colleagues told me that the guy got in through the front door, but he didn't break it. It still works. So he managed to override the lock. Surely that isn't an opportunist. That is someone with a plan.'

'Perhaps,' Phillips conceded, 'but it could still be someone who knows you. Forgive me, but you can look up how to break in through a door quite easily online.'

'So you're saying someone I've wronged planned their

revenge, looked this shit up, then broke in and cut me? Marking me with a goddamn occult-looking symbol. Sorry, I don't think I know any Satanists.'

DC Phillips sighed. 'You'd be surprised what people can really be like—what secrets they can hide, even though they appear perfectly normal to the outside world. I deal with this kind of thing all the time. So, could we please explore the possibility? Is there anyone you can think of who may have wanted to hurt or humiliate you?'

Kirsty didn't want to answer that, as she didn't want to push a line of thinking that she knew would follow through to a dead end. One name did spring to mind, of course.

Dom.

However, she knew for certain that he was not the man who had attacked her. She had seen the man's eyes, and they were not the dark, brooding eyes of her former boyfriend. The man who had raped her.

A small part of her thought about just giving up his name anyway. Telling the detective that, sure, it could have been her ex. But what would that accomplish? Even if he didn't have an alibi, and was charged for everything, then in a roundabout way he would be getting what he deserved, but the real attacker was still out there. And still free to do this to other people.

And Kirsty would still carry on seeing those... things.

'No,' she finally said. 'I can't think of anyone. Honestly. I don't really have many enemies.'

'No jilted exes or estranged family members that you have fallen out with?' he asked.

Kirsty shook her head. 'No. None.'

'Okay,' he said, but looked disappointed.

'Did you look into what the mark is on my back?' Kirsty asked, redirecting the conversation down the path she wanted. 'You sounded pretty dismissive of that before, but surely it's worth looking into?'

'We will look into it, Miss Thompson,' he said, 'I promise you. It's just... I don't think it's as significant as apparently you do. Again, I see lots of weird things doing what I do. Things that, at first glance, seem like they could be important, because they are too strange not to be. But, more often than not—actually, *always*—it is just unhinged people doing unhinged things for the sake of it. With no further meaning behind it. From the brief search I've carried out, there are no local incidents where anyone has reported being marked like you have.'

'What about farther afield? Why just search locally?'

'Because, at present, we have no reason to believe that it spreads any farther. It seems the man knew the area, and people who break into houses tend to do so in places they are familiar with. And, a lot of the time, there isn't much for us to go on.'

'Forgive me,' Kirsty said, 'but I get the impression this investigation is going to lead to a dead end. You don't seem very optimistic.'

'I'm just trying to be honest,' he said.

Their attention was then drawn to Amanda, who entered the kitchen. She now looked immaculate—her make-up perfect, low cut jeans, a halter top. The fearful girl Kirsty had seen in the bathroom was gone, replaced by the no-bullshit Amanda of old.

She had her armour back on.

'Hello,' DC Phillips said, greeting Amanda.

'Hi,' Amanda replied curtly. 'I take it you're the detective Kirsty told me about?'

'That's right,' he said.

'Any leads, then?'

'We are still working through a few things.'

Amanda just scoffed. 'So that would be a no.' She shook her head, moved over to the kitchen, and took out two cups. 'Would you like a drink, Kirsty?'

'Coffee, please,' Kirsty replied. She waited, but Amanda didn't offer one to DC Phillips, which Kirsty thought was deliberate. Kirsty held back a smile as the scruffy man shifted in his seat, looking a little uncomfortable.

'Well,' Phillips said, 'if there is nothing else, I'll be on my way.'

'Okay,' Kirsty said, 'but please keep me updated. I'd like to make sure the man who did this is caught.'

'We'll do our best,' he said, with very little enthusiasm. He hopped down from the stool and started to walk to the door, not waiting for Kirsty, who got up and followed him anyway. She opened the front door for him, and he stepped outside. 'Thank you for your time,' he said, setting his hat back on his head. 'We'll be in touch.' And with that, he walked away.

Kirsty shook her head and muttered under her breath, before walking back into the kitchen to see Amanda, who thrust a steaming mug of coffee into her hands.

'You weren't wrong about him,' Amanda said. 'He seems useless.'

'Tell me about it,' Kirsty said, taking a sip of her drink. Before the conversation could continue, Kirsty's phone—which was sitting on the breakfast bar counter top—vibrated and lit up. She walked over and grabbed it. A message displayed on the screen.

It looked as if she had a reply to her earlier post.

17

'WHAT'S GOT YOU SO ENTRANCED?' Amanda asked Kirsty, who was engrossed with her phone. Kirsty wasn't sure if she should tell Amanda what she'd been up to, but fuck it, Amanda wanted her to show fight, and her post was her way of doing just that. Kirsty wasn't about to wait around for that inept detective to turn anything up; she was going to do it herself.

And Amanda would have appreciated that, Kirsty knew, were it not for the fact that it was driven by not just a search for justice, but a desire to understand what was happening to her. The things she was seeing.

The message that had come through from Reddit was a direct one—not a public reply, but for her eyes only, from someone with the username ProfLBeckett. The message simply read: *I believe I can help you. I have seen this before. Reply, and I can share what I know.*

Kirsty tapped out her reply, eager for this stranger's help, leaving Amanda looking mildly irritated at Kirsty's lack of response.

If you can help, I would appreciate it. How can we best speak?

She hit send, and then set her phone down, only to see Amanda looking back at her with eyebrows raised.

'Well?' the blonde asked.

'Well... I've decided to take the bull by the horns,' Kirsty replied.

'And what does that mean?'

'It means that I want the man who did this found, and I'm not going to rely on anyone else to do it for me.'

'Wow,' Amanda said, a big smile crossing her face. 'I like the attitude, but how do you propose to track this guy down? Do you have any experience in private investigations that I don't know about?'

'Not really,' Kirsty said. 'But I do have access to the internet.'

Amanda furrowed her brow. 'What are you up to, Kirsty?'

Kirsty's phone vibrated again, indicating she had received another message. It was from ProfLBeckett, and read: *I'm set up to Skype if that works for you?*

Kirsty considered the proposal, and decided that it seemed safe enough. After all, it wasn't like she was giving a total stranger any information that could come back to haunt her. Given what had happened, the last thing she wanted to do was to hand another lunatic the chance to do something stupid, but what could he glean from a Skype call? She had a feeling Amanda would think it an irresponsible move, but this wasn't happening to Amanda. So, Kirsty typed out her reply: *that works for me. When is a good time to talk?*

She then turned back to Amanda. 'Don't get mad,' she said.

'Why?' Amanda asked. 'What have you done?'

Kirsty explained it all to her friend: the post on Reddit—including the photograph—and the subsequent response. Amanda, as predicted, was not on board with the plan.

'Are you crazy?' she asked, almost yelling. 'That is insane. What the hell were you thinking?'

'I was thinking that I want to find this man. I was thinking that I don't want him to get away with what he's done.'

'And you think this is the best way to find him?'

'It's the *only* way I can find him,' Kirsty replied. 'What else have I got to go on?'

'You still don't have *anything* to go on,' Amanda insisted. 'Even if you find out what this symbol thing means—so what? You still won't have your man. You still have nothing.'

'But it can't hurt to find out. It's better than sitting here and twiddling my thumbs. What harm can come of it?'

Amanda paused, thinking the question through. As she did, the phone vibrated again, but Kirsty kept her concentration on her friend this time. Amanda continued, 'I don't know. It seems weird, taking help from a stranger on the internet. You don't know this person at all.'

'His handle says Professor—'

'Oh, bullshit!' Amanda snapped, cutting Kirsty off. 'I could create a username saying Queen of the World; it wouldn't make it so.'

'Then I'll have wasted a few minutes of my life on a conversation,' Kirsty argued back. 'Big deal. It's not like I've got anything else planned. except sitting in my home, too scared to leave, in case I see anyone I know and have to tell them what has happened to me. At least this way I feel like I'm doing something!'

Amanda relented, softening her stance. 'Fine,' she said.

'I guess I can understand that. But I get to listen in, to make sure you don't say anything you shouldn't.'

'Fine,' Kirsty agreed. In truth, she would rather have the Skype call in private, without Amanda watching on, but there was no way that could happen with her in the house. Kirsty checked her phone and saw another message: *Give me a few hours to get back to my office. Would 3 pm suit?*

Accompanying the message was the user's Skype details. Kirsty suddenly felt nervous, but sent her reply: *Ok. 3 pm is fine. I'll call then.*

'Looks like it's on,' Kirsty said.

'When?' Amanda asked, arms folded.

'3 pm.'

Amanda checked her watch. 'This is fucking nuts.'

'Maybe, but I guess we have some time to kill.'

The two spent the next few hours not really doing a whole lot. They watched a little TV and tried a bit of small talk, but there was an anxious feeling in the air. Neither, it seemed, could settle. Amanda gave a few half-hearted attempts at talking Kirsty out of the call, but Kirsty would not be swayed. The memories of what she had seen, both in the hospital and last night in her bedroom, were fresh in her mind. The horrible memory of that man and woman, and the shadowy figure that always seemed to watch on, was constantly preying on her. Kirsty wanted—no, *needed*—answers. Hopefully, the upcoming conversation with the stranger would provide them.

After what seemed like an eternity, 3 pm neared. Both Kirsty and Amanda were watching TV in the living room when Kirsty got to her feet.

'It's time,' she declared and walked through to the kitchen. Amanda followed as Kirsty retrieved her laptop and set herself up on the breakfast bar, with Amanda standing beside her, yet just out of view of the built-in webcam. Kirsty opened the application and hit dial.

She felt her palms sweat a little as they both waited for the call to be answered. It rang and rang, and Kirsty cast Amanda a worried glance. Perhaps it was a prank, or maybe she was dialling a nutcase as Amanda had suggested? Maybe it would be better to just end the call now and forget the whole thing?

She didn't get the chance.

The call was answered, and a livestream image opened up on the screen, showing an older gentleman sitting in a chair in what appeared to be a rather grand-looking office. The walls were a deep red, blocked by a couple of mahogany bookcases. The webcam was not the best quality, lending a low-key atmosphere to the video. The man, who Kirsty assumed was the user ProfLBeckett, had white hair in a neat side part, with a matching well-trimmed beard. Despite the low lighting, Kirsty could make out the man's sparkling blue eyes that radiated a certain compassion and warmth. He gave a wave and a smile that came off a little awkward, but endearing.

'Good afternoon,' he said, 'thank you for calling me.' The man was well spoken, his voice having a certain aged, hoarse quality.

'Thank you for offering to help,' Kirsty replied, finding her own voice, but still feeling a little anxious about the whole thing. 'Can I ask, how come you've seen the symbol before? Do you know a lot about this kind of thing?'

'You could say that, yes,' the man said. 'Allow me to introduce myself. My name is Professor Lloyd Beckett, and I have a PhD in English language. But, in recent years, I've moved over into the research of occult practices and symbolism. Hence why I believe I can help.'

'Okay,' Kirsty said, wanting to look over to Amanda and say, *see, I told you he was a professor,* as her friend would simply counter with, *you still don't know that.* Which was true, of course. But Lloyd Beckett certainly had the look of an academic. 'My name is Kirsty, Kirsty Thompson,' she said, out of courtesy, if nothing else. A flurry of movement caught her attention as Amanda quickly waved her arms.

'You didn't need to give him your surname,' she whispered. Kirsty ignored her and concentrated on Lloyd.

'Pleased to meet you, Kirsty,' he said. 'Sorry about the circumstances. I understand you have been attacked?'

'That's right,' Kirsty said, realising she was going to have to go through the entire story yet again. This time, though, she kept it brief. 'A few nights ago, I came home and went to bed, as normal. I woke up during the night to find someone had broken into my home. He attacked me, drugged me to knock me out, and when I woke up I had the symbol cut into my lower back. The one I took the photo of.'

'That's awful,' he said, looking like the meant it. 'I am going to be honest with you, I only know a little about that particular symbol; however, I have seen it before in similar circumstances.'

'Similar how?' Kirsty asked, already feeling like she knew the answer.

'I don't know how to best put this... but it has appeared on people, in a similar fashion to the way it was—and please excuse the term—branded onto you.'

Kirsty's heart dropped at the revelation. 'Jesus Christ,' she exclaimed, trying to process the whole thing. Looking to her side, she could see that Amanda's expression had changed as well—mouth hanging open a little, and eyes wide.

'Quite,' the professor replied. 'I have seen a number of

cases—four, to be exact—but I am of the mind to believe there have been more.'

'You've seen them, what, in person?' Kirsty asked. 'You've met other people this happened to? Do you know who is doing it?'

Professor Beckett shook his head. 'No, I'm afraid not. I haven't actually met these people, but I have read reports. After coming across two similar incidents, I have been on the lookout for it happening again, to see if I can help.'

'How long has it been going on?'

'The first report I saw on this would have been in the late 2000's. 2009, I believe. It was in a local newspaper. Quite a story for the area I live in, back then. The next report was a few years later, and I came across it online. That one was many miles from where I lived. The other two were in different parts the country as well. Where are you based, if I may ask?'

'Knaresborough, near Harrogate,' Kirsty said, without even thinking.

'I know Harrogate,' he replied. 'A lovely place.'

'So,' Kirsty responded, 'were any of the previous attacks close to me?'

The man shook his head. 'Not particularly. They all seem to be quite spread out.'

'Okay. And did you reach out to these other women, like you did with me?'

Professor Beckett shook his head. 'I'm afraid not.' He chewed at his lower lip, clearly struggling with something.

'What is it?' Kirsty asked.

'Well, I don't quite know how to say it. First, it was not just women this happened to. A few victims were men. And also...' he paused again, 'in every instance that I saw the mark, the victim in question was... dead.'

Kirsty let out an audible intake of breath and covered her mouth with her hand. 'Dead?' she asked, the words slightly muffled through her hand.

'Unfortunately, it's true. The reports were all centred on what was believed to be murders, and this symbol was cut into each victim. Due to the scarring, it was believed the mark had been placed on the skin quite some time before death.'

'I don't believe this,' Kirsty said, suddenly feeling light-headed. The world around her began to swim. Her throat dried up and her palms dampened with sweat.

'Which is why, when I saw your post, I knew I had to contact you. Given my area of study, I've found the internet, and some message boards in particular, to be rich with information. If you can wade through all the misinformation, that is.'

Kirsty leaned back on her seat, almost forgetting she was perched on a stool with no back and came close to falling off the edge. She managed to grab the countertop and catch herself in time.

'I don't know what to do with that information,' she admitted. 'And the police have no idea who is behind it?'

'I don't believe so. I followed up each case I could find to the best of my ability, and not once did I find any closure.'

'So the man who did this is still out there?'

'If indeed it is one man. I suppose we can't be certain of that.'

'But you think it is?' Kirsty asked, sensing his tone.

'Possibly. Many of the details seem to be consistent, and each story, while newsworthy, certainly wasn't national news by any stretch. Can't imagine it would be a copycat or anything like that. Of course, I'm not a detective, you understand?'

Kirsty nodded. He may not have been, but in five short minutes this man had been more use to her than Detective Constable Phillips had been in days.

'So what else do you know? How long after the mark was cut into the victims did they die?'

'I'm afraid I can't say for certain. One of the reports said the cuts—as they called them—had scarred, so it would have been a few weeks to months I'd estimate.'

'Holy shit.'

'Have you contacted the police...' he paused, 'I'm sorry, is it Miss or Mrs.?'

'Miss,' Kirsty confirmed.

'Thank you. Have you contacted the police, Miss Thompson?'

She nodded. 'Yes, but I don't have a lot of faith in them. Did the others do the same?'

'I'd imagine so, but can't say for certain.'

'Can you send me any information you have? I can then pass it on to the detective looking into my case.'

'Of course, I'd be happy to. But, other than the reports in the newspapers, and several online articles, the only thing I have is what I know of the symbol itself. It's all quite super-stitious, so I don't know how much credibility the police would give it.'

Kirsty leaned forward. 'What is the symbol? Can you tell me about it?'

The man nodded. 'Of course. I like to think I have an extensive knowledge of symbolism and the occult, but this is something that I have not seen referenced very often. You can imagine, therefore, that things like this tend to be of the most interest. Other than the reports and, erm, murders, we have spoken about, I have come across this symbol only a few times before. Once, again quite recently, my sources told me there was a similar etching in a fire, in the North East of England. A house burned down, and two parents were killed. Only the children survived. Apparently, a similar mark was found in a mill that was on their land. This was where the parents were found dead, in rather horrific circumstances. That plot of land, it seems, had quite the history, so was of great interest to me.'

'You said similar?' Kirsty interrupted. 'So, not exactly the same?'

'No,' the professor said. 'Not exactly. There were a few differences, subtle though they were. The instances I have found of the same symbol, exactly the same, are from a document I have uncovered, though it's a copy, not an original.'

'A copy? Of what?'

'Well, it's hard to explain. Not many believe what I have is genuine, as they doubt the existence of the original. The copies I have are from pages of a document—or rather, missing pages of a document.'

'I'm confused,' Kirsty said.

'I don't blame you. I can ramble on and sometimes have trouble making myself clear, I'm afraid. There is a book, a fairly well-known book in my profession, that exists. Its existence isn't in doubt. However, in this ancient book, there are some missing pages. Many people have questioned why these pages were removed, and what exactly they contained. I believe the copies I have come to obtain could well be from those missing pages.'

Kirsty's head was reeling, and she was struggling to keep up. 'And what was the book?'

'Have you ever heard of the Codex Gigas?' Professor Beckett asked.

Kirsty shook her head. 'I can't say that I have.'

'And I can't say that I blame you, as it isn't very well known outside of academia. But it also goes by another name: The Devil's Bible.'

'Are you fucking kidding me?' The words were out of Kirsty's mouth before she had the chance to filter them.

'I know how that sounds,' Beckett said, holding up his hands defensively. 'And I'm sorry for being insensitive.'

'No, it's fine,' Kirsty said. 'I didn't mean to say that. It's all just a lot to take in, given what has happened recently.'

'I understand,' Beckett said. 'Or, at least, I can try to. I doubt anyone will really understand what you are going through. If I do say something too upsetting, please feel free to tell me to shut up.'

Kirsty managed a laugh. 'No, I don't think I'll need to do that. Believe it or not, this is actually quite helpful. So how come you believe these are the missing pages, then? How do you know there even are pages missing from this Devil's Codex thing?'

'Codex Gigas,' the professor corrected. 'It is well known that pages have been removed. The book itself is very old, with the consensus being that it was written in the early thirteenth century, in Bohemia, which is now the Czech Republic. It is a massive tome, containing many works, including the Vulgate Bible—'

'Vulgate Bible?'

'Yes, a fourth-century Latin translation of the Bible. There are many other works in the Codex Gigas as well, and it would have taken decades to complete. At least, it should have...'

'What do you mean, *should* have?'

'Well, legend has it—and this is just legend, mind you, there is nothing to really confirm it—that it was written by a monk. This monk had broken his monastic vows, and was sentenced to be walled up alive.'

'Nice,' Kirsty cut in.

'Quite. It seems men of God have a long history of doing things that seem, well, deplorable. Anyway, in order to avoid his punishment, the monk made an offer to his brethren: he promised that he would create for them a mighty tome that would glorify the monastery, and this is where stories diverge. Some say he promised it in one night, others a year, and there are other variations still, all with equally unachievable timescales. The story goes that the monk worked as hard as he could, but knew he would not meet his self-imposed deadline. Desperate, the monk then carried out a special prayer, summoning the Devil. He promised his soul in exchange for the book being finished. The Devil accepted, and then completed the book. Now, what is odd about the Codex Gigas is that, while it is very much a work that glorifies God, there are things within the work that are a little... strange. For example, a full page is dedicated to an image of Satan. Such prominence is odd in a work of God. And, of course, there are the missing pages. These were apparently deliberately removed, but when, and by whom, no one really knows. Again, legend has it that these pages contained what is known as The Devil's Prayer, as well as other incantations. I believe the copies I have in my possession are taken from the original missing pages of the Codex Gigas. This symbol, the one you are now marked with, was one of many within those copied pages.'

'Holy shit,' Kirsty said. 'That's a lot to take in.'

'I can imagine so.'

'So what does it all mean? Is the man who did this familiar with the Gigas Codex?'

'Codex Gigas,' Beckett said, correcting Kirsty.

'Fine, Codex Gigas. Does that mean this man knows about these missing pages? If that's the only other place you have seen the symbol, it makes sense that's also where he saw it. Perhaps he has the originals?'

'I'm not certain of that,' Beckett said. 'But, if I have copies, then there is a possibility he has them too.'

'So he's... what, just running around, saying this Devil's Prayer, and unleashing spirits and demons onto people?'

'Well, the symbol isn't actually referenced in the Devil's Prayer, not in the copies I have. That specific symbol is actually used in a separate incantation, but... I'm sorry, did you say unleashing spirits and demons?'

'Yeah,' Kirsty said. 'Isn't that what it's used for?'

'Well, kind of. I suppose that's the gist of it, yes. But, may I ask, how in heaven's name did you know that?'

Kirsty hesitated, not knowing how to best answer. Should she come clean, and explain what was happening to her? The man seemed understanding, but would that be a little too much, even for him? There was no telling if Professor Beckett actually believed in this kind of thing, or if his interest was purely academic. She looked to Amanda, who was unreadable. Kirsty had half expected her friend to jump in and cut off the call, given how things had gone, and how ridiculous the conversation must have sounded. But, with the apparent revelation of the mark's origin, Kirsty figured that Amanda was likely giving the Skype call some credence.

'It's kind of hard to explain,' Kirsty said, sheepishly.

'Well, I certainly don't mind you trying,' Beckett said. 'I'd be more than happy to listen. Were you aware of the Devil's Prayer and the symbol before our call?'

'No,' Kirsty said, shaking her head. 'Not at all. It's just, ever since that man cut this thing into my back, I've been having strange experiences.'

Professor Lloyd Beckett raised his eyebrows, and Kirsty also saw Amanda shake her head, obviously displeased at where the conversation was headed.

'What kind of... experiences?' Beckett asked.

'I've been seeing things. Things I can't explain. People. Dead people. And something else as well, something... that I can't really explain. I know how this sounds, and believe me, if I wasn't certain, I wouldn't tell anyone, but that's the reason I'm so desperate.'

Beckett didn't respond for a few moments and, when he did, he seemed unsure of himself.

'Okay,' was his only response.

'But it makes sense, right, given what you've said about these pages? If that's what this symbol is supposed to do, then wouldn't it all fit?' Kirsty was well aware of how desperate she was beginning to sound.

'Well, theoretically,' Beckett said. 'However, I have to be honest here, my interest in this is not from a paranormal point of view. In all honesty, I've never believed in such things.' Kirsty felt her stomach drop, and the man went on. 'So I've never given much credence to the validity of the rituals that I study. I am more interested in the reason they are followed and performed, and I endeavour to record their existence.'

'I see,' Kirsty said, suddenly feeling very stupid. She had thought the man might have believed her, and then she would finally have someone on her side.

'But,' Beckett said, 'given what I know about the previous cases, I do believe that you have every right to be concerned. If others who had this mark are dead, then, if I were in your shoes, I would try and get to the bottom of it all.'

'But I don't know where to start. And if no one believes me, then what am I supposed to do?'

'Well, you did go to the police. That's something.'

'Forgive me,' Kirsty said, 'but I haven't been very impressed with the police—not from what I've seen so far. If I have to rely on the detective I've been assigned, then I think you'll be shortly reading another report of a woman found dead.'

'I see,' he said, solemnly.

'I suppose I could tell them what you've told me, about the previous victims. They would have to look into that link.'

'You could,' Beckett said. 'Probably should as well. However, if I may be so blunt, it was always my theory that the person who marked his victims with these symbols had returned to finish them off, so to speak. Whether he saw that as the final part of the incantation or ritual, I'm not sure. But it was, to my mind, the only explanation. So, if they are no closer to finding this man, it might be worthwhile trying to find him yourself. And I say this as someone who is usually very averse to putting oneself in danger.'

'But I have no idea how to do that. I have no way of knowing who he was.'

'I understand,' Beckett said. 'And while I'm no detective, as I've said, to my mind a person like this would pick his victims carefully. He wouldn't just act on impulse for fear of being caught. He has been doing this for a long time, it seems. So, I'd wager he has been watching you for a while.' That thought caused goosebumps to form on Kirsty's arms. Beckett went on. 'So, is there anyone in your past you have seen, or met, that might fit the bill?'

'I don't think so,' Kirsty said. 'I see my friends and work colleagues all the time, and family every now and then, but that's about it. Other than people I pass on the street, I guess. But I can't remember all of them.'

'Okay,' Beckett said. 'But this person obviously knew you, or knew *of* you, and knew where you lived. And they were perhaps aware of the layout of the house, too. Is there anyone you can think of who could know all of this? A delivery driver, perhaps, or something of that nature?'

Something clicked in Kirsty's mind.

It wasn't a certainty, but a possibility. 'A year or so ago,' Kirsty said, 'I had a new alarm system installed. The man who came out seemed a little... well, awkward. Not very good with people. There was definitely something off about him. He was in this house for quite a while.'

'Okay,' Beckett said, leaning forward. 'And what did he look like? Anything that resembled the man who attacked you?'

Kirsty concentrated, trying to remember a man that she had not thought about in over a year.

Pale skin. Crooked nose. Blue eyes.

She gasped. 'Oh my God! It's him. I think it's him.'

Kirsty was shaking, and the revelation was difficult to process. Had she really just figured out who her attacker was? Amanda leaned in a little closer now, taking more interest.

'Very good, Kirsty,' Beckett said. 'You may well have taken a step forward here. And you are in a position that the previous victims were not, I'd wager.'

'I need to call the detective,' Kirsty said, feeling frantic. 'Thank you for the help, Mr. Beckett. I really appreciate it.'

'If I may,' the professor replied, 'there may be something else to consider.' He paused a little. 'I can't quite believe I'm going to say this, but I get the impression you aren't really one to lie.'

'What is it?' Kirsty asked.

'You told me that you've seen things since this happened to you? Can I ask, and please don't take offence, are you certain that what you saw was real?'

Kirsty took a moment to answer, conscious of Amanda so close to her. But she had no doubt in her mind. 'Yes,' she said. 'I'm certain.'

'Then that is troubling,' Beckett said. 'I wouldn't have believed it, but you pretty much verbatim described what the incantations in the missing pages were written to do. And without seeing it beforehand to know that... well, I'm struggling to find another explanation—beyond the fact that something is happening to you.'

Kirsty was a little stunned. Was someone finally taking her claims—outlandish as they were—seriously? 'So why should that stop me from going to the police?' she asked, but the answer dawned on her quickly, and she replied to her own question. 'Because I need to stop whatever he started,' she said. 'And I can't do that if he is in prison.'

'Quite,' Beckett said. 'I cannot believe I am recommending this course of action, but if it's true—and what he started with the attack is now taking place—then it will not actually be him that ends it. This thing that has attached itself to you is supposed to grow over time, and manifest itself more frequently as its link to our world grows. It uses the souls of its past victims, souls it has claimed, to help. Eventually, this thing would seek to claim your soul as well.'

'Jesus,' Kirsty said, slumping a little on her stool.

'And I really don't know what to advise,' Beckett said. 'Logically, it shouldn't be real. You should go to the police with what you think you know and let them deal with everything. But...'

'But, what if it's true?'

Beckett nodded. 'Exactly.'

Kirsty was silent for a long time. She cast a glance over to Amanda, who was looking serious and shaking her head at her friend. The gesture was clear: *don't even think about it*.

'Okay,' Kirsty said. 'You've given me a lot to digest. And I want to thank you, Professor, you've been an enormous help.'

'I hope so,' Beckett said. 'And if you need anything else, you know where I am. I'll help however I can. And, for what it's worth, I am so sorry this happened to you. The whole thing seems like madness, but you need to protect yourself, however you see fit.'

Kirsty nodded. 'I will.'

She then ended the call, and the dimly lit image of the kind professor blinked out. Kirsty turned to Amanda.

'We have to call the police,' Amanda said. 'Don't get any silly ideas, Kirsty. That professor was right about one thing —the whole idea of it *is* madness. Whatever happened, or is happening, is not paranormal or supernatural or any of that. But if you know who this man might be, we tell the police. They are the only ones who should be dealing with it.'

Kirsty got to her feet and walked over to one of the kitchen drawers. She pulled it open and started to rummage through.

'What are you doing?' Amanda asked, but Kirsty didn't answer, and instead kept on searching.

Eventually, she found what she was looking for—a small business card that she had kept for a year. Kirsty had stuffed it into the drawer after receiving it and had forgotten about it until now.

It was predominantly white, with frayed edges, blue writing, and a symbol of a sword in one corner. It was from a company called Spartan Security. On the card was a name and an office telephone number.

The name was Simon Bridges. Kirsty let a smile form over her lips.

Gotcha, you bastard.

18

'ABSOLUTELY NOT,' Amanda said, folding her arms over her chest. 'This is ridiculous, Kirsty. You need to get a grip.'

Amanda couldn't believe what her friend was proposing.

'It's the only way to find him,' Kirsty argued.

'No, it isn't,' Amanda countered. 'The *police* can find him with the information you are going to give them. And they can do it quicker than you can.'

'Who? That inept detective? You saw him, Amanda, he was beyond useless. How can we trust him?'

'Because it isn't just him,' Amanda went on. 'Yes, he may be the worst excuse for a policeman I've seen, but he isn't the only one. Hell, you could say you aren't happy with him and demand someone else take over.'

Kirsty shook her head. 'I'm making the call.'

'That's insane,' Amanda snapped.

'Fine,' Kirsty replied with a shrug. 'Then I'm insane. But I'm still doing it.'

Amanda closed her eyes and brought a thumb and fore-finger up to the bridge of her nose, pinching it as a headache started to form. How could her friend be so stupid? The call to that stranger—Professor Beckett—had been bad enough. It had, she supposed, actually been helpful in the end, given they now had a suspect, but then the conversation between the two of them had taken a strange turn. Kirsty had again pushed the issue of the things that she claimed to have been seeing. The things that were clearly just in her head. And the fact that she now believed in those things meant that she wasn't thinking rationally. And worse, now it seemed like Kirsty was going to actively obstruct the police's investigation by trying to do things herself.

And she was going to make a mess of everything in the process.

Amanda was sympathetic, to a degree, knowing that her friend was struggling. Hell, she herself had been on the cusp of letting her imagination run away with itself after the incident in the bathroom, so she knew how easy it was. But that was in the heat of the moment. Amanda was thinking clearly now, and she wouldn't be scared by make-believe. There were no such things as ghosts and nothing in the shadows haunting them. She refused to believe it was true, as her mind simply wasn't set up that way. It would completely wreck her belief system, her whole understanding of reality. And the thought of that happening was, in and of itself, terrifying. So, seeing Kirsty going farther down that rabbit hole worried her. Amanda knew she had to guide her friend back to sanity.

But Kirsty already had the mobile phone in her hand.

'Please, Kirsty,' Amanda said, practically begging her friend to see sense. 'Just stop and think about it. We want this guy caught, and if you get yourself involved, it could mess everything up.'

Kirsty seemed to consider her words for a moment, but then shook her head.

'No,' she said. 'This man involved me when he broke into my house, cut me, and set these things onto me. I know you don't believe me, but I believe it, and I'm going to do something about it.'

With that, she began to dial.

19

SANDRA COLLINS PICKED a loose bit of fluff from her navy-blue skirt and wiggled her fingers, dislodging it, then watched as the lint drifted down to the floor. She was perched on her chair at the reception desk, and it had been a long, slow day for the secretary. There had been painfully few calls, and that—coupled with the lack of paperwork and filing to be done—meant the thirty-three-year-old had been left bored. That, in turn, had caused her mind to keep running back to her bastard of an ex-boyfriend, who had run off with a twenty-something with fake tits only a month ago.

That, after all Sandra had done for him. She'd even put her own studies and career ambitions on hold, dropping out of her course and taking this routine job so that he could concentrate on his career instead. And for what?

To be dropped at the first sign of interest from a younger model. And now she was stuck, both in her personal life and in a dead-end career.

The chair she sat on was a high one, allowing her to sit level with the tall reception desk—a laminate pine table that she kept in neat order. The front office she worked in by herself was small and lonely, containing only her desk—with her computer and phone on top—and a side table that held an old, redundant fax machine. There was also a solitary window directly ahead, one that looked out over the small car park in front of the building. Beyond that lay the dull, colourless industrial estate beyond.

Sandra shifted in her chair, and it squeaked below her. The patterned blouse that was part of her work uniform was not the most comfortable, and the heels she was wearing were starting to chafe. Sandra let them fall to the floor and wiggled her feet and toes, enjoying the feeling of freedom. Sandra looked at the clock and sighed; she still an hour or so to go, which would drag, and no doubt feel like an eternity—when all she wanted to do was to go home and have a nice big glass of wine. Perhaps she'd even look into the possibility of re-starting her forensics degree, to once again follow her passion. It would be difficult to do now, given the amount of time that had passed, as well as the fact she was reliant on her mind-numbing job—but that didn't mean it was impossible.

She jumped a little as the phone rang for the first time all afternoon. Grateful for the distraction, Sandra lifted the handset and brought it to her ear.

'Good afternoon, Spartan Security,' she said, 'Sandra speaking, how can I help you today?'

'Hello,' a female voice replied on the other end of the line. She sounded a similar age to Sandra, but a little unsure of herself—something Sandra was used to with the people that phoned in. Most of the calls she fielded were either from potential customers looking for quotes, or people needing help with a recently installed system. The girl went on. 'I had an alarm system fitted by your company about a year ago. The man who installed it said he would help with anything I needed. I know a little time has passed, but wondered if it was possible to speak to him, to ask him a few questions?'

'Well,' Sandra replied, politely, 'I may be able to help you. Can I ask the nature of the problem?'

'Actually,' the woman said, almost hesitantly, 'I would prefer to speak to the man who installed it if that's okay?'

'Certainly,' Sandra said, feeling a little annoyed, but doing her best not to show it. Did this person think she was incapable of helping, just because she was a secretary? Sandra had suffered stereotyping from callers before—but she let it go and carried on with the call. 'Can I take the name? All of our engineers are out at the moment, carrying out installations, but I can get one to call you back.'

'Yes, his name was Simon Bridges.'

Sandra had to think about that for a moment, then her mind caught up and she felt her skin crawl a little. Simon hadn't stayed with the company for very long—a few months or so—and had left almost a year ago, not long after the installation of this lady's system, it would seem. Sandra had never liked the guy and always found him creepy—in fact, she had caught him on more than one occasion watching her in the office, just staring at her when he didn't think she was looking. And besides that, there was something decidedly off about the man.

'I'm sorry,' Sandra said, 'Mr. Bridges no longer works for Spartan Security.'

'Oh,' the woman said, sounding disappointed.

'I can try and help, or get another engineer to contact you, if you'd like? I'm sure that whatever the problem is, it's something we can get resolved for you.'

The woman paused. 'Is there any way to contact Simon Bridges? I really need to speak to him.'

Sandra raised an eyebrow. Why in the hell would anyone want to speak to *him*?

'I can't really help with that, I'm afraid,' Sandra said. 'Simon left a while ago, and I'm not able to give out any of his private information that we have on file. I'm sure you can understand.'

However, it seemed the woman did not understand at all. 'It's very important I speak with him,' she said, starting to sound a little distressed.

'I'm sorry, ma'am,' Sandra repeated, 'but there is nothing I can do in that regard.' She was trying to remain professional, but got the feeling that this call was not really about alarms or security systems. And, if Sandra was honest with herself, she was more than a little bit curious as to what was really going on.

There was a brief silence on the line, one Sandra was tempted to fill, but the woman spoke instead. 'Can I be honest with you?' she asked.

'Of course,' Sandra replied.

'Well, after Simon came out to see me, we kind of kept in contact. We met up a few times and things started to get... a little serious. Well, at least I thought so.'

'Okaaaay,' Sandra said, trying to give her mind time to catch up with what she'd just heard. It was a very interesting twist on an otherwise boring day.

'The thing was, he always came to see me. I don't even know where he lives. And a few months ago... I found out that I was pregnant.'

'Oh,' Sandra replied, and things started to fall into place for her. It was now obvious why the woman was trying to track Simon down. Sandra suspected he had run out on the girl and abandoned his responsibilities. 'I see.'

'After I told him, he just disappeared. Didn't return my calls and just ignored me. I've been trying to find him for months. I don't have any family to rely on and...' the woman's voice cracked, and she started to sob. 'I'm scared,' she said. 'I don't know what to do and I don't know if I can cope.'

Sandra listened to the woman cry on the other end of the phone, and her heart broke for the poor girl a little. She wanted to help, to make sure that horrible little weasel didn't get away with leaving the woman—the mother of his child, it would seem—all alone.

But she couldn't. While Sandra didn't remember seeing an actual company handbook that would cover such matters, she was almost certain that doing something like giving out personal details to a strange caller was a sackable offence. But the woman went on.

'Please, if you could just give me Simon's address I can go and visit him. Hopefully make him see sense. I won't tell anyone who gave me the information, I swear.'

Sandra clenched her teeth. It would be simple enough for her to do: all employee details—past and present—were stored on the company database, which she had access to via her computer. And the likelihood was that no one would ever find out.

But there was always that risk, because all calls at the company were recorded, and Sandra could ill afford to lose her job. She felt torn.

'I'm really sorry,' Sandra said, her voice soft, trying to sound understanding. 'But that's not something I can do. Is there no other way to get his address? Are you not acquainted with anyone else who knows him? His family or friends?'

'No,' the woman said. 'He was very private. I realise how this sounds, but I knew next to nothing about him. I thought he'd eventually open up, not just dump me when I needed him.'

Fucking men, Sandra thought, happy to tar them all with the same brush at that moment, fair or not. She could relate to the woman a little, given how her own ex had treated her —dropping her when she was no longer wanted or needed.

But if Sandra gave out the info, and for some reason word did get back to her employers, they only had to check the call logs. Then she was done.

It would surely be enough to get her sacked.

Sandra looked at the display on the base of her desk-phone and saw that the caller was using a mobile phone. The number was displayed on the screen and, upon seeing it, an idea formed. She made a note of the number.

'I'm really sorry,' Sandra said again, at the same time pulling up the company's database. She found Simon Bridges' information and scrolled down to the address they had on file. 'But there is nothing I can do. I am going to have to end the call now.'

'Wait,' the woman said, but Sandra replaced the receiver. She felt bad, but she had done what she felt she needed to. At least half of it. Sandra then took a breath and tapped the address into a text message. Alongside it, she typed a note: *I hope you find him and make him own up to what he's done. Please don't tell anyone where you got this.*

Then, Sandra hit send.

20

'THAT,' Amanda said, 'was pathetic.'

'It was worth a try,' Kirsty replied, wiping away the fake tears she'd conjured up. Perhaps her friend was right, maybe she had gone too far in trying to con the poor secretary like that.

Amanda shook her head. 'I'll give you this, you're a hell of an actress. But, can we drop it now and call the police?'

Kirsty let out a sigh, feeling frustrated and defeated. Before she answered, however, her mobile phone vibrated. She snatched it up and opened the text message that had just come through from an unknown number.

She read the message.

'Holy shit,' Kirsty said.

'What now?' Amanda asked.

'It's from the woman I just spoke with.'

'And?'

Kirsty smiled and looked up to her friend. 'It's the address. She sent me the address.'

'You're kidding,' Amanda exclaimed and looked at the screen as well. 'Fuck.'

'This is good,' Kirsty told her. 'It's what we wanted.'

'No,' Amanda argued. 'It's what *you* wanted. But let me tell you something, we are *not* going to that address.'

'Well, you might not be,' Kirsty shot back, 'but I am.'

Amanda shook her head, and actually looked a little sad. 'No, you're not.'

'You can't stop me, Amanda.'

'I'll just call the police myself, and tell them everything.'

Kirsty stared daggers at her friend. 'You wouldn't.'

'I'm sorry, Kirsty, really, but I just want you to see sense. Don't you get how dangerous this is? What could happen to you if you go?'

'I know it's dangerous,' Kirsty answered, 'but it's the only option I have.'

'Why?'

'You know why.'

Amanda rolled her eyes, causing a shot of anger to surge through Kirsty. 'Stop with that rubbish,' Amanda said. 'How many times do I have to tell you, none of it is real.'

'How can you be so sure?' Kirsty asked.

Amanda shook her head as if confused by the question. 'Because they don't exist, Kirsty. You know that.'

'No, I don't know that. Not anymore.'

Amanda threw her arms up in the air, exasperated. Kirsty knew they were not going to reach any kind of agreement on their issues: both going to the man's address and the existence of things beyond their understanding.

Not that long ago, Kirsty would have sided with her friend on the second issue, but things were different now. And there was something else that Kirsty was curious about —before the detective had arrived, earlier that morning, Kirsty had heard Amanda scream from the bathroom. After running up to check on her, Kirsty saw that Amanda had looked terrified. Amanda had said it was because... what was the reason, again? That she had gotten the towel caught around her head?

Kirsty hadn't believed it at the time, but had taken her word for it. Now, however, it seemed like Amanda really was protesting the existence of the supernatural a little too much. Perhaps, Kirsty thought, Amanda was simply trying to convince herself, as well.

'What happened up in the bathroom, Amanda?' Kirsty asked, changing the course of the conversation, and clearly catching her friend off guard.

Amanda paused and her expression dropped slightly, if only for a moment, before she regained herself. 'What do you mean?'

'When I came up, after you yelled, you looked scared shitless. What made you that way?'

'I wasn't scared shitless,' Amanda said, gritting her teeth. Kirsty had obviously touched a nerve. 'I told you what happened,' Amanda went on. 'I got the towel stuck and panicked a little because I couldn't breathe.'

'How the hell does someone get a towel stuck around their head?' Kirsty asked. 'I saw your face afterwards, Amanda. You were scared of something. And I mean *really* scared, not just panicked.'

'No,' Amanda said, defiantly, 'you're projecting. You're only seeing what you want to.'

Kirsty didn't believe that, but knew she wasn't going to get anywhere. Amanda had her guard fully up now, and there wasn't time to bring it down.

'Look,' Kirsty said, deciding to change tactics. 'I'm asking you—no, *begging* you—as a friend, just let me do this.'

'But it's—'

'It's dangerous,' Kirsty interrupted. 'I know that. But it's something I need to do. You don't have to come with me if you don't want to, but I need you to let me do it. I *have* to see him again, to look him in the eye and find out what all of this is about.'

'But why not let him go to jail? Surely that's the best outcome.'

Kirsty shook her head. 'Not for me it isn't. I need to know, Amanda. It's the only thing that will help me get through it. You say all of the things I've been seeing are in my head? Fair enough, maybe they are. If that's the case, then this will help me.'

'Kirsty, did you forget about those other people? The ones with the same mark? They're all dead. If you go to him, and he's the one who killed all those people, then you're only giving him the chance to finish the job.'

'I don't think that's true,' Kirsty replied as calmly as she could.

'How can you say that?'

'Because I'm not waiting for him to come for me. I'm taking things into my own hands and going on the offensive, and he won't be expecting that. I thought you would understand, given you were so keen for me to defend myself.'

'Kirsty, there's a difference between learning a few self-defence moves and actively going looking for trouble.'

'Amanda, please, I need this.'

Amanda was silent as her eyes bored into Kirsty's, and Kirsty could practically see the cogs ticking over in her mind. 'If you're going,' Amanda said, 'then I'm going too.' A big grin broke out over Kirsty's face; however, Amanda held up a finger. 'But,' she said sternly, 'we go tomorrow.'

'What? Why?' Kirsty asked.

'Because it's almost five o'clock,' Amanda replied. 'We don't even know how far that address is from here. I'd prefer to do a little research first, find out where it is, and then head over tomorrow when we are more prepared. Plus, I'll see if Mike can make it as well. I'd feel safer if he was there.'

Kirsty felt a knot form in her stomach. If Amanda's new guy was going to be there, that meant they would have to tell him everything—and Kirsty really wasn't comfortable with that. For one, other than the police, the only person she had told about Simon's attack was Amanda. Kirsty hadn't even told her parents yet, so why should a man she'd never even met get to find out before them? And then she would have to explain to Mike the real reason they were going to Simon's house, rather than to the police. They would need to explain the conversation with Professor Beckett, the Codex Gigas, and the things Kirsty had been seeing. And Kirsty was well aware how she would come across to someone with no real context.

They would think she was crazy.

'No,' Kirsty said. 'No Mike. I'll wait until tomorrow if you want, but I don't want anyone else knowing.'

'It'll be safer,' Amanda repeated. She had a point, Kirsty knew that, but Kirsty just didn't think she could face the judgmental stares of someone else finding out about her.

'Sorry, but no,' Kirsty insisted. 'Like I said, I'll go alone if I have to, but I don't want anyone else knowing about what happened. Not yet. I'm just not ready. Look, I promise, after we find the man who did this, and find out what it all means, we go to the police.' She prayed Amanda would see it her way, but her friend would not relent.

'But how are we going to make him talk? Did I miss the part where you were trained in interrogation? I mean, we don't know for certain that this is our guy—we're only going on a hunch. This is way out of our league, Kirsty. But if you want him to talk, then Mike is our best chance. So, how about you see things my way for once? You want this freak to talk, and find out what it all means, then Mike is your best shot.'

There was a silence. Kirsty seated herself on the stool again, feeling her legs grow weak. As much as she hated to admit it, she knew her friend was making a lot of sense. Could the two of them really go to a dangerous person's house and force him to spill everything? More likely, they would both end up dead, like his other victims before them.

Amanda was right; they needed help, which Amanda's boyfriend could provide. And that meant Kirsty would have to tell him. And, once she did, there was no guarantee he wouldn't just dismiss the story, call her a freak, and demand they do the right thing and leave it to the police.

'Would he even help us?' Kirsty asked. 'I mean, it's a pretty big thing to ask of someone.'

Amanda just smiled. 'Leave that part to me. I'll have no problem getting him on board. Trust me; he'll make this fucking weasel talk.'

Kirsty gave a slow nod. 'Okay,' she said. 'We go tomorrow. And Mike goes with us.'

Amanda moved to the other side of the breakfast bar and sat down opposite her friend. She put a hand on Kirsty's forearm. 'Then, afterwards, we go to the police and get this fucker put away for good. Sound like a plan?'

'It does,' Kirsty said.

'Good. Now, I'm going to go and speak with Mike. You pull up Google Maps and see where the hell that address is. I want to know where we're going. The more information we have, the better.'

'Okay,' Kirsty replied. She got to work on her laptop as Amanda stood and walked to the kitchen doorway.

'Give me a few minutes,' she said and left to the room to

make the call. Kirsty heard her enter the living room and close the door behind her. Kirsty would have liked to know what Amanda was saying, a little fearful of how her friend would make her sound, but instead concentrated on what she needed to do.

She typed the street name into her computer and hit search. The satellite view orientated itself over a built-up area in a nearby town. Kirsty could see that the street in question was a terraced one with a line of houses on each side, facing each other. She clicked on the Street View option, and the screen then switched to an image of the street from a first-person perspective.

If the view here was still current, and she had little reason to believe it had changed much since the shot was taken, then the street looked quite run down. Many windows on the small, terraced dwellings were boarded up, and the cars in the long street were old and beat-up.

Kirsty used the arrow option on screen to move the view forward, virtually walking down the road. She kept rotating as she did, looking at each side of the street, trying to find a house number on the doors to orientate herself. She saw one and zoomed in. The screen was blurry, but Kirsty was sure the small numbers were a three and a six. She was in the mid-thirties, and the house she was looking for was number sixty-seven.

As Kirsty worked, she heard the muffled sounds of Amanda's voice from the other room, though it wasn't clear enough to make out exactly what was being said. She pushed the view forward again on the screen, moving farther down the street and seeing the numbers increase on the doors as she did. Eventually, she found the one she was looking for.

Number sixty-seven.

The house had a pebble-dash render to the walls, and the doors and window frames were timber—the white paint flaking, exposing the wood beneath. Kirsty could also see dirty netting up in the windows, blocking the view inside.

This was the house.

A couple of doubts ran through her mind; the first, and most important being, was this really their man?

He was a strong suspect, given his knowledge of Kirsty's house, and the alarm system that he himself had installed. And it was suspect that he had seemingly left his job not long after visiting Kirsty. But did that really mean anything? All that she had to go on was the vague memory of what he looked like, and those certain features that she was comparing to her attacker, specifically the eyes and nose. At first, she had been sure, but now she wasn't, and doubt began to creep in. What if she was making a horrible mistake, and was about to accuse an innocent man?

There was another potential issue as well; this was the last known address Spartan Security had on file, Kirsty assumed. But, given how long it had been since Simon Bridges had left, what was to say that he still lived here? They could all be about to roll up and find someone completely different living there. Though, she figured, if that was the case, then at the worst it would just be a wasted trip. And perhaps she could find out where Simon Bridges had moved to.

After studying the house for a little while longer, and finding nothing else of interest, Kirsty checked the Route Planner, plotting the course between her own address and Simon's. The computer showed the drive over would take approximately forty minutes, which was quicker than she had been fearing. While the trip would probably seem like a lifetime, as nerves would likely build and take over, she knew it could have been much worse.

With little else to look for, Kirsty explored the map further, checking out alternative routes and looking at adjacent streets—killing time until Amanda was finished. Before long, she heard the voice from the next room go silent, then the door opened, and Amanda returned to the kitchen.

'Well?' Kirsty asked.

'He'll help,' Amanda told her. 'Took a little convincing, but if the guy we're going to see is our man, Mike will make him talk. He'll call around here tomorrow morning.'

Kirsty nodded. 'Thanks,' she said, not sure how to feel.

'No problem. Now, how about we try and take our mind off things and just enjoy tonight as best we can. A little wine, perhaps?'

Kirsty let herself smile. 'Sounds good to me.'

The two girls opened a fresh bottle and tried to unwind.

The night had other plans.

21

AMANDA'S MIND swam back into consciousness, and it took her a moment to remember where she was: in Kirsty's spare room.

Her head hurt and her throat was dry—last night's wine having its undesired, but unavoidable, effects. She squinted her eyes, looking through the dark around her, to the source of light that, she assumed, had awakened her. From the doorway of the room, Amanda saw that the landing light was on, and the door open. Amanda couldn't even remember for certain if she'd closed it—she assumed she would have, but perhaps Kirsty was up using the toilet and had peeked in to check on her? Amanda listened, but could hear nothing.

She rolled back over and closed her eyes, hoping to ignore the light, but found it futile. While it wasn't particularly bright, the glare that seeped into her room was enough of a nuisance to keep her from getting back to sleep.

'Goddamnit,' she muttered to herself and swung her legs out of bed. She stood and gave herself a minute to balance herself, given the hangover and grogginess that had made her lightheaded, then made her way over to the door. She peeked out onto the landing, expecting to see the bathroom door to be closed, with Kirsty inside. It was open, with the light off. Perhaps Kirsty had finished her business and gone back to bed, but left the landing light on? Amanda listened and heard light snoring coming from her friend's room.

She stepped out onto the landing and flicked off the light, plunging everything into darkness. Amanda then closed the door to her room and dragged herself back to bed, letting herself fall into it. She pulled the covers tightly up to her chin and closed her eyes, waiting for sleep to once again claim her.

But she could not relax, suddenly aware of a pressure on her bladder. She sighed, annoyed she hadn't taken care of that while she was up. She debated trying to ignore it, but now that Amanda was acutely aware of the need to pee, the sensation seemed to be growing.

'Goddamnit!' she repeated, with more venom this time. Amanda threw the covers back and got up out of bed again. But, once up, she paused when looking over at the door to her room, seeing light from the landing seep in from the small gap at the bottom.

The light was on again.

Amanda felt a small tightening of her chest, and the first hint of fear creep into her subconscious, pushing away the grogginess.

Don't get carried away, she told herself, not wanting to get sucked down the same road of fear and paranoia that Kirsty was currently barreling down head-long. Amanda needed to be the voice of reason. Even though, she had to admit, it was very easy to frighten oneself once that tiny seed of doubt had been planted.

'Kirsty?' Amanda called out, a little timidly. There was

no reply. She shuffled over to the door again and, after taking a breath, slowly pulled it open. She looked outside, to see the landing light on again, but no one present. All was quiet, as it should be. Perhaps it was a problem with the light fixture or wiring? Amanda stepped farther out and turned her head to the light switch. She had flicked it down when previously turning it off, but it was up once more.

No problem with the light fixture or wiring, it seemed—someone had flipped the switch.

Calm, calm, calm, she told herself, fighting to keep the memories of her experience in the bathroom at bay.

This time, rather than switching the light off, Amanda crept over to Kirsty's room, as another notion presented itself. It was entirely possible that it was her friend doing it, whether subconsciously or not. Amanda had no idea if Kirsty sleepwalked, but that could account for things. In fact, that made a whole lot of sense—she'd heard of a certain kind of terrifying dream before, one that seemed very real to the person experiencing it. Night terrors, they were called, and maybe that was what Kirsty was experiencing.

Amanda had seen accounts of people who suffered from those dreams, and she'd read that the people in question were in a state halfway between sleep and consciousness—which is why it felt so real. Given what Kirsty had been through recently, that line of thought was beginning to sound more and more plausible to Amanda: that all of what Kirsty was seeing, and the reason it seemed so real, was because her brain was half-awake when seeing it.

And if Kirsty sleepwalked as well, perhaps she had flicked on the light... twice. Amanda shook her head, realising that part seemed a little far-fetched. However, had Kirsty not flicked the light on in her sleep, perhaps she had done so on purpose in an attempt to scare Amanda and make her believe. Amanda was aware that was also a bit of a leap, and she felt bad for thinking it, but knew it was possible. She'd seen how easily and convincingly Kirsty had lied when on the phone with the secretary.

Amanda opened the door to Kirsty's room as quietly as she could and poked her head inside. Kirsty lay on the bed, her chest slowly rising and falling as she breathed; her head moved from side to side, and Amanda could see that she was sweating. Kirsty gave off an unsettled moan. The covers from her bed were flung back, bunched at the foot, no longer over Kirsty's form.

Again, Amanda felt bad for thinking this way about her friend, but what other explanation was there?

'Kirsty?' Amanda whispered. Kirsty continued to breathe, rhythmically, and if she had heard Amanda, she made no show of it.

Amanda watched her friend for a few moments, then turned to leave the room, and in doing so—and in her tired state—slammed her shoulder against the leading edge of the open door. The sharp corner dug into her skin and pain rippled from the line of impact.

'Fuck!' she yelled out instinctively.

As she gripped her shoulder, Amanda heard Kirsty draw in a breath. The girl sat up in her bed, opening her heavy eyes, and made eye contact with a shocked, wide glare. Kirsty shrieked in fright.

'It's just me,' Amanda said, still rubbing her shoulder. Kirsty squinted her eyes, then a look of realisation drew over her.

'Amanda?' she asked. 'What are you doing? You scared the hell out of me.'

'I was just checking on you,' Amanda replied.

'Why?'

Amanda thought quickly. 'I was just up using the toilet, and I wanted to make sure you were okay. I was just about to leave and hit my shoulder on the door. Sorry for waking you.'

A warm but tired smile formed on Kirsty's face. 'It's okay,' she said with a yawn. 'Thank you for doing that, but I'm fine.'

'You looked like you were having a bad dream.'

Kirsty nodded. 'Yeah, I think I was. I've been having them ever since the attack.'

'Which is understandable.'

'I guess,' Kirsty answered. There was a pause between them, with Amanda unsure of what to say next. Eventually, she spoke.

'Well, since I've made a good job of waking you up when you were sound asleep, I'm gonna head back to bed and leave you in peace. Sorry again.'

'It's fine,' Kirsty said with a tired laugh.

Just as Amanda was about to turn, however, the light from the landing outside blinked off again with an audible *click*.

Amanda felt her heart freeze.

'What was that?' Kirsty asked, her voice shaky. 'Did the light just turn itself off?'

Amanda was slow to reply. 'Don't panic,' she said. 'It's been happening every now and again. Faulty wiring, I think.' But even though Amanda spoke the words, and tried to sound convincing, she didn't believe them.

She took a step outside of the room and peered into the darkness.

'Don't go out there,' Kirsty said, but Amanda did anyway. She had to.

She couldn't see anyone in the shadow of the night, and other than the girls' own erratic breathing, she could hear nothing. If there was someone—or something—else around, they were totally silent.

Amanda moved farther out onto the landing and peered over the bannister, down the stairs. Yet again, all was clear, and she heard Kirsty get out of bed and approach from behind, pressing herself up against Amanda, hugging her in fear.

'It's okay,' Amanda said, though the sound of her own voice betrayed what she was really feeling. The silence around the pair almost seemed to make things worse, and Amanda just wished that if something were going to happen it would just happen, rather than this anxious waiting. And, as if to answer her wishes, both girls heard something.

A thunderous noise from all around them—three sharp bangs, sounding as if someone was striking the water pipes of the house. Amanda let out a quick shriek as Kirsty gripped her tightly.

'What is that?' Kirsty asked as a silence once again resumed. Even so, Amanda felt like she could still hear the loud crashes. She searched her mind for a rational explanation, but did not get the chance to come up with one.

Three more bangs rang out, this time sounding even louder. Amanda yelled out again in fright and held on to her friend. There was no rational explanation for this at all, she knew, and the fear she was trying to keep in check began to rise and take hold.

Another three crashes, the loudest yet. Both girls screamed as they stood hugging on the landing, burying their face into each other's shoulders, attempting to hide themselves.

They stayed this way for a while, panting in terror,

waiting for further disturbances. No other banging was heard after the initial three sets of three, but soon, another noise came to prominence.

It was a sound laced with evil and intent. A cackle, from downstairs.

22

YET AGAIN KIRSTY found herself gripped by a terror that shook her to her very core. The two friends stood hugging and trembling on the landing, and Kirsty hated the fact that, in the last few days, this kind of fear had become all too common to her.

And yet it had grown no more bearable.

The sounds that had crashed around them had been bad enough, but the sinister laugh that she had just heard downstairs sent a further icy chill through her veins.

'This is fucking insane,' Amanda said.

'What do we do?' Kirsty asked, feeling as lost and scared. How were they supposed to deal with something like that? What was the best course of action? Bolting from the house seemed the most appealing option for her, but that meant leaving the safety of her friend's embrace and making their way downstairs—and who knows what would be waiting for them down there.

'I don't know,' Amanda admitted.

Then they heard that damn cackle again. It continued

for a while, before eventually morphing into a long, pained moan. It was accompanied by a distinctive sound, something sliding along the tiled floor in the entranceway downstairs.

Kirsty wanted to run back into the bedroom and hide under the covers—anything except face whatever the fuck was moving downstairs. To her dismay, however, Amanda had a different tactic in mind. The blonde untangled herself from Kirsty and stepped towards the bannister again, looking down the flight of stairs. Kirsty didn't even have time to tell her friend to get back when Amanda gave a sharp gasp and slapped a hand over her mouth. Even in the dark, Kirsty could see Amanda's eyes were wide with fear.

Kirsty couldn't help herself and didn't know what kind of morbid curiosity motivated her, but she had to see what Amanda was seeing, and what had freaked her friend out so much. They were both sharing the experience, so Amanda could no longer bury her head in the sand about it. And if her friend had seen the same kind of thing Kirsty previously then they were now in this together. So she leaned in, next to her Amanda, and looked down... and immediately wished she hadn't.

Thanks to a small stream of illumination from the streetlight outside that shone in through the glass of the front door, Kirsty was able to see the figure that slowly crawled forward, pulling its body along the tiled floor.

The woman was old and had wild, wiry hair. She was face down, so at the moment Kirsty had no idea what she looked like, but the frailty was obvious due to the skinny limbs that poked through the dirty white nightgown, making the woman's advanced years clear to see. The skin—pale, with bulging purple veins—was wrinkled and creased, and bony arms and legs worked together in a crawling motion that seemed to take great effort as her extremities shook with exertion. The moaning from the woman continued as she moved—a long, low, haunting sound, one of pain and misery. The ghastly woman then reached the bottom of the stairs and began to turn herself.

Kirsty tried to pull Amanda back. 'We need to run,' she said, but Amanda would not budge. The blonde still had a hand over her mouth, and her eyes were still wide from terror—practically bulging out from her skull—but the girl watched on nonetheless, rooted to the spot through a mixture of terror and fascination.

Kirsty looked back down and saw that the old woman was now starting to pull herself up the stairs, still keeping her head low and face down.

She was making her way up to them.

'I... I don't believe it,' Amanda said. 'It's real. It's all real.'

Thoughts of *I fucking told you so*, surprisingly weren't at the forefront of Kirsty's thinking, because all she wanted to do was to get away from that fucking thing.

The old woman climbed the first few stairs, her body moving a little quicker this time, with a little more agility, as she found the stairs an easier terrain to move across. Then, she stopped, and slowly lifted her head. Now, Kirsty was able to fully make out that horrible face.

The skin on the woman's head was pulled tight, showing the outline of the skull beneath, and she had dark, drooping eyes, the exact colour of which Kirsty was unable to spot given the limited light, but even so, she could see that something was wrong with them, and knew that they contained that damn symbol lining the fleshy orb. The woman also had a long, hooked nose, one that almost fell over a mouth that hung loosely open. Kirsty felt the darting eyes fix on both her and Amanda.

The old hag then smiled.

But it wasn't a normal smile. The sinister grin that pulled itself open was far too wide to be natural, the teeth behind jagged and blackened.

The cackle returned, and the woman then moved quickly, scuttling up the stairs like a spider. An awful clicking sound accompanied her lightning-fast movements, and somehow the woman had made it halfway up before Kirsty and Amanda managed to overcome their terror. They soon snapped back to reality, however, and sprinted back into the bedroom. As they broke through the threshold of the door, and Kirsty turned to slam it shut, she saw that the old woman was somehow right behind them, crawling rapidly along the ground of the landing. Kirsty tried close the door, but, as she thrust it halfway shut, an unknown and unseen force heaved it back open, pushing Kirsty back a few steps in the process.

The crawling nightmare scuttled into the room, and that vile clicking sound continued to ring out as she moved. Kirsty and Amanda—screaming the whole time—jumped over the bed to the other side, putting the wide piece of furniture between them and that... thing. It was little in the way of an obstacle or deterrent, but it was all they had.

From their standing position, Kirsty and Amanda saw the old woman hold her ground on the other side of the bed, crouched down, ready to pounce. She still wore that unnatural smile on her wretched face. And when she did move, it was not to attack, as Kirsty had expected; instead, her movements were slow and deliberate as she began to take off the nightgown that covered her torso.

The woman slipped the material up and over her head, casting it down below to the floor, out of sight, and letting the two girls take in the sight of her gnarled and mutilated body.

One breast, limp and dangling, hung down towards the centre of her stomach. The other was missing, cut away, showing a black and decayed pit in the flesh instead. Deep cuts and gashes covered most of the skin, some a dull red, others black and pulsating with a dark liquid. She opened her legs and allowed the thick, dark thatch of hair that covered her sex to be revealed.

Another cackle.

The woman then turned, her movements slow and, strangely, quite graceful. Kirsty and Amanda could now see her back, where there were more cuts and scars lining the skin. However, there was one marking that was so clear and large that it dominated the rest and immediately drew the attention of Kirsty and Amanda. It was something Kirsty recognised.

The mark.

The same one Kirsty now had on her own skin.

The ragged lines of the woman's symbol were bright red, as if the flesh beneath was still live and raw, in contrast to the dead meat on the rest of her. After the reveal, the woman turned around again and held out an arm. A long, bony finger extended, pointing directly towards Kirsty.

Yet again, she let out that horrible laugh.

Kirsty understood the meaning, and her frightened mind jumped back to her conversation with Professor Beckett, specifically to the missing pages of the Codex Gigas.

It uses the souls of its past victims.

That's what the woman was, once: a past victim, now made a demonic servant for the darkness behind this whole thing—the entity Kirsty had seen when the spirits manifested, watching from the swimming shadows.

Which meant it was likely looking on right now, as well.

The old woman opposite them once again started to lower herself into a crouched position, then continued down, pressing her stomach to the floor and laying out flat. She pushed herself up on arms and feet, readying herself to crawl towards them.

Kirsty stepped back, with Amanda following suit, pressing themselves into the wall behind them. Kirsty felt the window sill dig into her lower back, causing an explosion of pain from her own mark.

The woman then moved, with frightening speed, and darted forward, arms and legs scuttling quickly, always accompanied by that clicking sound. She quickly disappeared under the bed; a fit that should have been a difficult one proved easy for her to slip through.

The clicking sound instantly stopped as Kirsty, screaming now, dropped to her butt. She had her feet raised high, ready to plant her soles into the woman's face if she emerged from behind the white valance that hung down to the floor. Kirsty waited, poised... but the hideous old woman didn't emerge. Amanda dropped down next to Kirsty and, slowly, reached out a hand to the cotton sheet that blocked their view.

'What are you doing?' Kirsty asked, incredulous. Amanda didn't answer, but instead grabbed a handful of the sheet and, in a quick motion, yanked it up.

The woman was gone.

Both girls simply sat, unmoving other than to breathe heavily in an attempt to control their fear. 'I don't fucking believe it,' Amanda said again. It gave Kirsty a small bit of comfort to know that her friend had actually been able to see those things as well. But comfort could wait. First, they needed to get the hell out of this room. And, it seemed, Amanda agreed.

'Come on,' the blonde said, getting to her feet and pulling Kirsty up with her. She grabbed Kirsty's phone from the nightstand and thrust it into Kirsty's hands. Amanda then quickly scooped out some clothes from Kirsty's wardrobe— jogging bottoms and a t-shirt—and dropped them into Kirsty's arms as well. 'We need to get out of here.' She then dragged Kirsty from the room and into the spare bedroom, where she grabbed her own phone and the bag she had brought with her. Kirsty was terrified, and it surprised her to see that Amanda was level-headed enough to use what time they had—however long that may be—to grab the essentials.

Clearly, they were leaving the house.

Once they had everything bundled together, the two girls ran from the room and down the stairs. Kirsty dropped her phone as they descended and watched it bounce down each and every step, before seeing it clatter across the tiled floor near the entrance, where it then skidded to a stop. They quickly reached the bottom, almost slipping while barefoot on the cold tiles, and Kirsty scooped up her phone. The screen had cracked, but it still illuminated. She hoped it would at least be usable.

Amanda tried the front door, but found it locked.

'Keys!' she demanded. Kirsty's mind was a blank at first, and it took her a moment to remember where she usually kept them.

'In the kitchen, second drawer down,' she eventually said, and turned to head off that way, moving slower than Amanda had done when leading the charge, well aware something could be waiting for them. She padded over to the kitchen, scanning the dark from for signs of... *something*.

She neared the drawers and cast a quick look out of the kitchen window into the back garden. It was dark outside, as well, with the moon above the only source of light, weak as it was. Then Kirsty did a double take, certain she'd caught sight of something outside.

She had.

Standing centrally in her garden was a naked woman, roughly Kirsty's age, with the same white skin as the other spirits Kirsty had seen—this one also mutilated and disfigured. The woman was waving, slowly, arcing a withered arm from side to side. Her most striking feature, however, was that she had no jaw, and her tongue lolled down past her throat.

'What the fuck is that?' Kirsty screamed.

'Jesus fucking Christ!' Amanda yelled before she pushed past Kirsty and pulled open the second drawer, quickly finding the keys. They both then ran from the kitchen, back to the front door, where Amanda slotted the key into the lock, fighting with it until the lock eventually clicked open. She was turning the handle when that familiar banging rang out again: three strikes.

Kirsty and Amanda spun around. A voice sounded, seemingly coming from everywhere and nowhere at the same time.

'*Soon,*' it said. It sounded unnatural, sexless and pained.

Kirsty and Amanda fled outside into the night with the spare clothes and bags still bundled in their arms. They did not stop running until they left the street, and then the housing estate completely.

It took them a few minutes before they started to think rationally again, and, still in a slight state of panic, Amanda called her boyfriend, hoping he would come and get them. Given the hour, however, she was unable to get an answer.

Instead, she managed to call and book a late-night taxi. 'We're going to my house,' she told Kirsty after the call. Kirsty didn't argue, but deep down knew it wouldn't be safe there either. She knew, after her hospital visit, then the experiences in her own home, that the entity would always follow her, no matter where she went.

23

When Kirsty opened her eyes the next morning, she felt like she had been dragged through hell. Though faintly aware that there was something happening around her, Kirsty's body just screamed at her to go back to sleep and get some more rest. She was currently experiencing a level of exhaustion she had not known before, so could do nothing but close her eyes again.

Kirsty was at Amanda's house, in her friend's spare room, tucked up in bed. Daylight forced its way into the room through the closed curtain, so she pulled the thick cover up and over her head.

There was a banging sound.

Not the terrifying noises from the previous night—this was different. It was normal. Someone was knocking on the front door, over and over. Kirsty could also hear Amanda quickly moving around.

'We overslept,' she heard Amanda yell, followed by thudding footsteps on the landing. 'That's Mike.' A pause, followed by, 'Kirsty, you awake?'

She was, but she didn't want to be. Her eyes were heavy... so, so heavy.

Just a few more hours, please.

Even the terrifying experience of last night would not dissuade her from sleep, nor the nightmares that would likely be waiting for her. And, despite everything that was going on, Kirsty actually felt herself doze back off.

But it was short-lived as she was violently shaken awake. In anger, she threw the covers back and sat upright.

'Goddamnit, Amanda, I just want...'

Kirsty trailed off as she realised she was alone in the small room. She could hear voices downstairs—one was clearly Amanda's, but the other was deeper, presumably that of Mike.

So who the hell had shaken her?

Kirsty's room contained only a single bed, with all walls except one decorated magnolia. The far wall, the one that contained the door, was painted a light purple. A few pictures were dotted around the room, which Amanda had taken herself, and had been blown up onto canvases. There was a close-up of some flowers, with a sharp focal point on the petals to draw attention and the green foliage blurred in the background, as well as some famous monuments, including Whitby Abbey. There was also a small bookcase filled with fiction books—mainly thrillers—and a night-stand. Other than that, there was nothing... and no one, with nowhere for anyone to hide.

Perhaps the shaking had just been a natural convulsion of her body? Like when you suddenly feel like you're falling when dropping off to sleep.

Regardless, she was suddenly very eager to get herself up and go downstairs to join the others. Throwing on the clothes she had grabbed the previous night, she quickly ran to the bathroom to freshen herself up as best she could.

Kirsty ran downstairs, all the while fighting the feeling that she was being watched. She was nervous about going down to meet Mike for the first time, knowing she was about to make a terrible first impression: *Hi, I'm Kirsty. I know we haven't met before, but I appreciate you helping me to go intimidate a stranger who may or may not have attacked me a few nights ago. But it's the only way I can get these damn ghosts to leave me alone, you see. So, yeah, thanks for the help!*

He was going to think she was a lunatic.

The one saving grace, however, was that Amanda had witnessed these things now as well, so there was no way she could deny the experiences any longer.

Kirsty timidly walked into the living room to see her friend dressed in tight jeans and a t-shirt that was deliberately a little small. Her hair looked a touch messy, which was unheard of for Amanda, and she appeared tired. Amanda was seated on the couch and, beside her, there was a large man with a shaven head and serious, dark brown eyes. He was well-built, with tattoos covering his arms, and Kirsty could see his muscle definition through the light grey t-shirt he wore.

Mike smiled at Kirsty, and she was surprised to see such a kind, warm smile from such an intimidating-looking person. He stood up and held out a large hand.

'Kirsty, I take it?' he said, with a voice softer than she expected.

'Erm, yeah,' she replied, feeling embarrassed. But she took his hand, and he gently shook it.

'From what Amanda tells me, sounds like you've been through hell.'

Kirsty nodded. 'You could say that.'

'And you are sure that this is the guy? Because you know how much trouble we could get into by doing something like this, right?'

'We're sure,' Amanda said from her position on the couch.

'Okay,' Mike said. 'And you're sure the police aren't best placed to handle it?'

Kirsty was about to answer, but Amanda did that for her. 'Yes,' she said, sounding a little curt. 'We're sure about that, too. Look, Mike, this is the only way. The police are useless, and this guy is going to get away with what he's done. We need help here, not more lectures and questioning. Are you going to help us, or not?'

Mike looked a little wounded, and Kirsty felt bad for him, but it was a change to see Amanda in agreement with her. Last night had clearly taken its toll.

'What she means is,' Kirsty cut in, attempting to smooth things over, 'we can't see any other way to deal with this, stupid as it sounds.' She kept her voice kind and gentle. After all, the man was helping them do something that was, well, unorthodox, to say the least. Possibly even breaking the law if they had to get... persuasive. Kirsty couldn't blame Mike for wanting to know as much as possible and to make sure they were doing the right thing. It was clear he was only doing this for Amanda, anyway. But sniping and talking down to him wasn't likely to cultivate his favour. Kirsty went on: 'The police have been no good at all, and I'm worried that if we tell them about this Simon Bridges, they'll screw it up. The thing is, they have no evidence to go on, they've already told me that, so how would they press charges?'

'Just to be devil's advocate,' Mike said, 'how can you be

sure it is him, then, with no evidence to back it up? Did you see his face? If so, couldn't you just identify him?'

Kirsty shook her head. 'He was wearing a mask. All I had to go one were his eyes, and a bit of his nose, I suppose. It is enough for me to be sure, but I don't know if it'll be enough in court.'

Mike nodded, seeming to understand. 'I get that. Sounds like an easy one for him to deny without you getting a proper look. But there is always the chance that it might not actually be him, you understand?'

'I know,' Kirsty said. 'I do. But when I see him again, I'll know for certain.'

'Okay,' Mike said. 'There's... one other thing that Amanda mentioned.' He sounded hesitant, and Kirsty knew exactly what he was referring to. The undead elephant in the room.

'The things I've been seeing?' Kirsty asked.

Mike gave an embarrassed smile and nodded. 'Yeah, that would be it.'

Kirsty looked to Amanda for support here—considering her friend had now seen the same things that she had—but Amanda turned away, face red, with a look halfway between shame and fear. Kirsty contemplated demanding Amanda back her up, but decided against it. This was hard enough for Kirsty to deal with, and she'd a few days' head start to process it all, so she knew exactly what Amanda was struggling with.

'I know how it sounds,' Kirsty said. 'Really, I get it. It sounds fucking crazy. And maybe it is all in my head, but at the moment it's real to me. And if we get this guy, and I find out the meaning of the symbol he cut into me, then maybe it will put my mind to rest.'

That was only partly true. Kirsty didn't for one moment

believe it was just in her head. Maybe after the first experience in the hospital that might have been true, but not now.
Not after everything she had witnessed.

'Symbol?' Mike asked, clearly confused.

Kirsty looked to Amanda. 'You didn't tell him about
that?'

Amanda shook her head. 'No, not really.'

Kirsty wasn't sure if she should have been annoyed by
the omission or not. If Amanda had seen fit to tell Mike
about the things Kirsty claimed to have seen, then why leave
out the occult symbol that the attacker had marked her
with. Surely, that should have been part of the story?
However, Kirsty ignored it, and instead turned around,
pulling up her shirt and removing the old dressing that
badly needed changing anyway.

She figured showing Mike what the attacker had done
would likely have more effect than telling him.

'Holy shit!' he exclaimed, proving her right.

'Yeah, that pretty much sums it up.'

Though she had her back to Mike, and therefore
couldn't see him, she could almost feel his gaze burning into
her, into that unsightly mess on her back. The one that
would, no doubt, leave a hideous scar that would be with
her for life. Kirsty didn't like the feeling.

'Okay,' Mike said, 'let's go and have a word with this
fucker.'

Now *that* was music to Kirsty's ears.

Kirsty and Amanda quickly showered and changed, and
the three of them got going—all bundled into Mike's car as
he drove.

Kirsty felt nervous but hopeful.

She prayed that, after confronting Simon Bridges, she

would find a way to stop what was happening to her—that all of this would then be over.

But deep down, Kirsty couldn't shake the feeling that things were about to get worse.

24

MIKE CALLAGHAN WAS FAR from comfortable with what he was doing, and the sensible part of him was screaming inside, telling him that this was insane. But another part of him, the protective part—the same one that had put a man in hospital after he had assaulted Mike's sister—was out for blood.

At first, he thought he was doing it for Amanda, perhaps as a way to impress her by looking out for her friend. Then, Mike had seen what the attacker had done to Amanda's friend, and that changed things. That got him angry. There was little in this world that infuriated him more than cowardly men who had to impose themselves onto people they considered weaker, just to try and claim some misplaced sense of dominance. Even now, driving towards their destination in his black BMW, Mike felt his blood boiling.

He checked his rearview mirror, seeing Kirsty in the back seat looking pensive. He felt for her and what she'd been through. Given the seemingly occult nature of the symbol she bore—and the no doubt fragile state of mind she would be in—it was hardly surprising she had scared herself so much that she thought she was seeing things. Such was the distress that this fucking prick had put her through. Behind Kirsty, following a few hundred metres further back on the road, he spotted a dirty white transit van, one Mike thought had pulled out of Amanda's street at the same time they had.

He shook his head, realising his anger was making him paranoid. It probably wasn't the same van at all, but even if it was, they had followed the main road out of town, so it wasn't strange for them both to be taking the same route.

Mike checked the Sat-Nav, which showed another twenty minutes left on the journey. The drive had been a quiet one so far, and the anxiety in the air was almost palpable. The droning radio did little to alter the mood.

Mike turned it down. 'So, what's the plan when we get there?'

Amanda turned to him with a blank look, and then turned to look back to Kirsty, who just shrugged.

'I guess we just knock on the door,' Amanda said.

'As good as any plan, I guess,' Mike replied. 'And what do we say?'

'Well, Kirsty needs to figure out if this is our guy,' Amanda said, turning back to her friend again. 'What do you think?'

Kirsty remained silent for a moment, her head slightly cocked. Eventually, she spoke. 'I go and speak to him alone. You guys keep out of sight.'

'What do you mean?' Mike asked, surprised. He thought the whole point of him coming along was to intimidate this freak.

'I want to face him first, to look into his eyes,' Kirsty said. 'I need to know it's him. If the three of us are all standing at the door, I doubt he'll say much. We might even make him panic and cause him to run.'

'Well,' Mike said, 'to be honest, he could run as soon as he sees you. He'll think he's been caught.'

'Possibly,' Kirsty said, 'but I'll try to act natural, like I'm there for some other reason.'

'Which would be?'

'I don't know yet. Maybe that I'm lost and need directions? Or that I'm selling stuff door to door.'

Mike wrinkled his nose. The plan sounded like a bad one. 'I don't know,' he said. 'Doesn't sound like it would work. Would you be able to just act natural, especially if it's the same guy?'

'You'd be surprised,' Amanda cut in, and Mike noticed Kirsty shoot her a scowl.

'I just need to see him on my own first,' Kirsty said. 'I need to face him.'

'And you can do that with us by your side,' Mike told her.

'I know that,' Kirsty said. 'And I want you by my side. You two will just hide beside the door and keep out of sight. There is no way he would let all three of us into his house. If I can talk to him a little, I might be able to get him to let me inside. That's when we all burst in. Because I don't really think this is something we can argue about on the street. A neighbour could call the police and ruin everything.'

Mike still didn't think it was a great plan, but at least they would be close by, to intervene if anything happened.

'Okay,' he said. 'We'll try that. Amanda? You okay with that?'

Amanda continued staring straight ahead, out of the front window to the road ahead. 'Yeah. As long as it puts an end to everything.'

She sounded dreamlike, as if her mind was far away.

AMANDA WAS STRUGGLING.

Last night had scared her, sure, but it had also affected her on a much deeper level, too. She felt like her world—her whole reality—had crashed down around her, and she didn't know what was real anymore.

The previous day, immediately after the incident with the towel in the bathroom, she had been terrified, certain that some unnatural force had attacked her. She even remembered hearing something at the time. But, after it had happened, Amanda quickly gathered her wits and thought rationally—or what she thought was rationally—telling herself to get a grip. It was all in her head, put there by Kirsty's outlandish stories. And after rationalising it, Amanda was comfortable with her explanation. In her reality, despite the wobble, everything was as it should be.

But then last night happened, and she had seen those things herself. There was no denying it anymore, and no *thinking logically*, as her experience the previous night could not be explained.

They were real.

That meant that the way she had viewed the world—her very belief system—had been wrong. It was such a monumental thing that Amanda, naturally, was having trouble coming to terms with it.

But now, above all else, she just wanted it all to end. She couldn't face another night like the previous one again, and the thought of seeing those things, potentially, for the rest of her life was beyond terrifying. Last night, she had experienced a level of horror that she had never encountered before, and it was not something she thought she could ever get used to. And that would mean living a life of fear—something she could not allow.

Amanda had no idea if things would stop if she distanced herself from Kirsty, but, ashamed as she was to admit it, the thought had crossed her mind. Ultimately, she'd dismissed the idea, but as they drove towards the home of Simon Bridges, she found herself praying that this was the right person and that Mike would be able to force Simon into making everything stop. The discussion with the professor the previous day, one she had initially thought of as outlandish and unbelievable, was now one she could not stop thinking about. That ancient text, the Gigas... whatever it was called, the missing pages from it—it seemed like fiction from a bad story, and yet here she was, right in the middle of it.

And she believed it was all real.

It was amazing how much life could change in such a short space of time. And not in a good way, either. Knowing what she now did, Amanda would give anything to go back to living in blissful ignorance.

'We're almost there,' Mike said, pulling Amanda from her thoughts. She felt her chest tighten.

'Okay,' Kirsty said from the back seat. 'Don't park too close to his house. We don't want him to see us coming.'

They turned into a long street, with terraced houses lining either side. The area looked neglected and miserable. Quite a few of the houses seemed empty, or abandoned, with boards covering windows and doors, and some of the cars that were parked were even up on bricks, stripped of their wheels. Mike's BMW would stand out like a beacon in a place like this, summoning the more undesirable elements to it. Amanda just hoped that by the time they got back, Mike's car wouldn't have been vandalised or broken into.

Mike pulled the car to a stop and Amanda saw the netting in the window of the house they parked outside of twitch a little. There was also the shadow of a figure moving behind—it seemed someone had spotted them already, so they would have to move fast.

Mike cut off the engine and turned in his seat. 'Are we ready?' he asked.

Amanda nodded, but the truth was that she felt anything but ready.

Kirsty took a deep breath, then spoke. 'Yeah, I think we're ready. Remember, I want you two to keep out of sight, just to the side of the door. Let's try the softly, softly approach first.'

'And if that fails?' Mike asked.

'Then we kick his fucking door in,' Amanda replied.

25

As she walked down the long street, Mike and Amanda a few paces behind her, Kirsty had a hard time keeping her nerves in check. Her heart was racing, and she could feel her palms become wet and clammy. The realisation of the situation—and the apparent absurdity of it all—hit her like a brick to the head. If this all went wrong, then she could very well have destroyed any chance that existed for the man to be caught and punished for his crimes.

But, of course, that wasn't the ultimate goal for her. What Kirsty wanted—no, *needed*—was for Simon Bridges to put a stop to the horrific things she had been seeing and experiencing. Kirsty needed the entity that had somehow attached itself to her to be gone for good.

If these experiences had been confined to her house, Kirsty could have just moved—a simple solution. Sure, there would be issues with regards to not being able to go back to her own home anymore, but at least she could get away from the immediate danger that manifested itself.

But that was not what was happening. The experience in the hospital had been the first one, and the entity had then followed her back home. It wasn't Kirsty's house that was haunted... it was *her*.

The trek along the street seemed to take forever, which on the one hand was a good thing, as it delayed the inevitable—something Kirsty wasn't sure she was ready for. But, conversely, it also allowed the anxiety and nervous energy to keep building to the point Kirsty felt like she was about to throw up.

Soon enough, however, a door she recognised came into view. The one she had seen on the computer earlier when looking at a street view of the house.

Number sixty-seven. The home, she hoped, of Simon Bridges.

Eventually, they arrived, and Mike and Amanda took their places beside the door—hopefully out of sight. Kirsty felt herself physically shake.

Get a grip, get a grip, get a grip.

She couldn't allow herself to look scared and nervous when Simon answered, as that would give the game away completely. She needed to be strong. Kirsty looked to her right, to the window, and saw that the curtains were drawn. She stepped back and gazed up to the first floor, noticing the windows on that level were covered over as well. Perhaps he wasn't home, or still in bed?

Or perhaps, given what sort of man he was, he didn't want anyone from the outside world looking in on him and the disgusting things he did.

Well, buddy, the outside world is here now. It's come knocking.

She took a deep breath, held it, then exhaled slowly, somehow finding the strength to steady herself. She lifted her hand and knocked three times on the door.

Kirsty waited for a full minute, at least, but she could

hear no movement within. Perhaps they had timed it badly, and Simon was out—if anyone even still lived in this house. Considering the state of some of the properties in the area, there was a good chance this one could now be empty as well. And if that was the case, then the only lead they had to stop what was happening would disappear.

She knocked again, harder this time. Another agonising wait, but with the same result. No answer at all.

No. No, no, no.

Desperation began to seep its way into her newfound calm. She knocked again, this time even harder, feeling the small shred of hope she'd held on to extinguish itself.

Then, thankfully, she heard it—movement from within. And next, there was an audible sound of someone fiddling with the lock. It clicked.

Then, slowly, the door pulled open... and there he was.

It took Kirsty a moment to take in all of his features, and the first thing she noticed were his pale blue eyes staring back at her. She felt her throat go dry.

This was their man.

Those were the eyes she had seen that night. And in them, she saw a look of recognition slowly form. Then they widened in alarm.

It was clear that he had recognised her, as well.

'Hello there,' Kirsty said, trying to sound as natural as she could. But, given how her voice cracked after the first word she spoke, thanks in no small part to the dryness in her throat, Kirsty knew she sounded anything but natural. Regardless, she pushed on, stating the line she had practised over and over again in her mind on the journey over here. 'I'm just in the area collecting for charity—for sick children, to be precise—and wondered if you had a few minutes to spare? I'd love to come in and go through the different ways you can help those less fortunate than your-self. Would that be okay?'

Kirsty had no idea if it would work. And, if he did invite her in, then what? She couldn't do this alone, and needed to get Mike and Amanda in there with her. But she knew that if they had all been standing outside on the doorstep when Simon had answered, he would have slammed it in their face.

She cursed herself for acting on such a half-baked plan in the first place. Why hadn't they thought of something better? Simon just continued to stare at Kirsty, and she had no idea if she'd managed to fool him.

'No.'

Then the door was slammed shut, and Kirsty again heard the sound of the lock working. She shook her head and looked over to Mike and Amanda, who stood a few yards away. Amanda mouthed the words; 'Was that him?'

Kirsty nodded and gave a thumbs up. She then turned back to the door, not ready to give up just yet. She would make him listen to her, and she had an idea of how to do it.

SIMON WALKED QUICKLY to the living room and began to pace back and forth, biting at fingernails that had already been mostly chewed away.

Fuck, fuck, fuck.

How had she managed to find him? This had never happened before. It shouldn't have happened now. He had been so careful, and was certain he'd left behind no evidence tying him to what he'd done. So, if that was the case, how had she tracked him down? And more so, how come it was the girl standing at his doorstep and not the police?

He didn't like it.

She'd said something about charity, but Simon knew a lie when he heard one, especially one so obvious. She was here for him, he had no doubt of that.

Fuck.

He searched his mind, trying to think of exactly where he'd messed up, but came up short. He'd left nothing behind that would lead back to him, he was sure of that. And how in the hell had she found out where he lived?

He should have moved on well before now, and cursed himself for getting comfortable. Normally, after marking his victim and infusing them with his tainted blood—the ritual that set the curse in progress—Simon moved away from the area. He would have run, but he had grown complacent recently. Well, perhaps complacent was the wrong word.

He had grown *tired*.

Tired of living a life like this, of doing the things he did, of what he *had* to do to survive. Simon knew he couldn't go on like this forever, but then, what other choice did he have? He hated what he was, what those people had made him, and he hated what he had to do to his victims and the curse he set upon them.

The thing that always claimed their lives... and souls.

But, in the end, it was them or him. And he hadn't asked for any of this madness. It had all been thrust on him, against his will.

But now his latest victim was here, on his doorstep. She'd done what no one else had yet managed. She'd tracked him down.

His breathing was rapid as his mind raced for a course of action to take. Only one presented itself.

Run.

He would run upstairs, gather some essentials, and flee —get far away from here as fast as he could.

Then he would wait for her to die. He would know when it had happened, too, which would mean starting all over again.

He had no choice.

The sounds of loud knocking on the front door boomed out again. Rapid, hurried crashes that did not cease. He worried that the commotion would draw attention. Then there was another sound, that of a voice, yelling through his letterbox.

'Simon,' the girl yelled. *Fuck, she even knows my name.* 'Let me in. I need to speak with you.'

There was absolutely zero chance that was happening. He tried to ignore her, instead concentrating on his escape plan. Where would he go? His old car was outside, parked on the street, but he would have to run past the girl to get to it. He wasn't the biggest guy in the world, but was confident enough he could overpower her, at least long enough to get into his car and get the hell out of there. It was an option.

'Simon,' the girl repeated. 'If you don't let me in, then I swear to God I'm going to create a scene. And I'm going to call the police and get them down here straight away. I'm going to tell them you're the one who attacked me—that I'm at your house right now and I need help. And I'm going to cut the tires of every car on this street so you can't go anywhere. If you don't open this fucking door now, then the police are going to come and arrest you. You're going to jail, Simon. You're fucked. But if you open the door and talk to me, that doesn't have to happen. It's your choice; you've only got until the count of five. I'm already dialling the police number as we speak, so hurry up and decide.'

Simon felt a huge weight on his chest, and he yelled out 'Fuck!'

What was he supposed to do now? If the police came and he was arrested, then it was all over for him. He wouldn't be able to carry out the ritual again once Kirsty was gone, and that meant he wouldn't be able to redirect the darkness towards someone else. It would be with him permanently. And that meant a short life of fear and terror for him—one of pain and suffering.

Then death.

But that wouldn't be the end. Death was only a step. There would exist an eternity more of pain and suffering, beyond what his mind could comprehend. And there would be no escape from that existence.

'One,' the girl shouted. 'The phone is ringing, Simon.'

He pulled at his greasy hair, hard enough to draw clumps free. His scalp stung and throbbed as he tugged at more. Frantic, he tried to look for a solution, but none presented itself. He didn't have time to run upstairs and get anything together. Should he just flee out of the back door?

'Two,' she yelled.

Perhaps he should just run out the front, as originally intended—overpower her, jump in the car, then drive off. It could work, if she hadn't already slashed his tires. But then she would have his registration plate and could pass it on to the police. It then wouldn't take them long to hunt him down.

As much as he hated the thought, the only feasible course of action he could see was to agree to what she was demanding. To let her in to talk. Once it was just the two of them inside, then he would have time to reassess and formulate a plan. He realised that in his frantic thinking, he had lost count of what number the girl was up to.

'Right,' she yelled. 'Time's up.'

He ran to the door, unlocked it, and pulled it open. 'Don't—' he yelled, then stopped short.

She was not alone. Another girl was with her—one he didn't recognise. They were accompanied by a large, shaven-headed man as well. And it was that man who stepped inside and shoved Simon back, causing Simon to lose his footing and topple into the stairs behind him. The man towered over him as the girls ran in behind, shutting and locking the door.

Simon felt weak. His world, he knew, was about to come crashing down around him. Before he could stop himself, tears started to form in his eyes and roll down his cheeks.

'Save the snivelling,' the large man said. 'We've got a lot to talk about.'

26

MIKE LOOKED DOWN at the cowering man on the ground.

He didn't know what sort of person he had been expecting to meet, yet the look of this pathetic rat didn't surprise him one bit.

This was Simon Bridges: thin, with a long, bent nose and a gaunt face. He had scraggly, wispy tufts of hair on his face, but not enough to be classed as a beard. Purple bags hung under tired-looking eyes, and he was dressed in dirty, ripped jeans and a stained t-shirt that hung off his slight frame. To Mike, this guy could have passed for a drug addict, which, if true, wouldn't have been a shock.

Mike bent down and grabbed Simon, taking a handful of the shirt just below the neck. He heaved the weasel of a man to his feet, and Simon let out a pathetic cry as it happened. Mike then brought Simon's face close to his own. The guy stunk—a mixture of sweat and weed—but Mike tried to ignore it.

When Mike spoke, it was through gritted teeth. 'Get in the fucking living room and take a seat. You've got a lot of explaining to do. And if you don't answer every question we have to my satisfaction, then you won't have to worry about the police, because I'm going to break every bone in your puny fucking body. Understand?'

Simon wasn't looking at him, instead just staring down to the ground, like a naughty, crying child. He kept sniffling as he sobbed. The sight of the man disgusted Mike—happy enough to force himself on unsuspecting women and drug them to have his way. Not strong or brave enough to try anything on someone bigger than him. Simon Bridges was nothing but a coward. Mike was having a hard time holding back, and not unleashing his anger and ripping the guy's fucking lungs out.

'I said, do you understand?' Mike shouted. Simon winced, but this time nodded. 'Good,' Mike said, and practically threw him through the threshold into the messy living room. Simon scuttled onto a worn-looking chair and pulled his knees up to his chest as he continued to snivel.

The room itself felt both sparse and cluttered at the same time. It contained only the chair Simon sat in, a sofa, and dirty clothes that were strewn about the floor. There were also piles of old books, and Mike noted that many of them seemed concerned with the occult, religion, and even some self-help paperbacks regarding finding forgiveness and self-worth. There wasn't even a television. The smell in the room was thick with the musty aroma of marijuana.

Mike took a seat on the sofa, though he didn't really want to. It was high-backed and uncomfortable, with a pea-green covering that had worn patches and stains from God-knows-what on its surface. He made himself as big as possible, popping his chest out and drawing his shoulders back, trying to be as intimidating as he could. Not that this man would take much to scare.

Amanda and Kirsty joined him, the three of them filling

the space on the sofa. Before he spoke again, Mike turned back to the window and considered opening the curtains. The dull bulb above didn't help illuminate the room much, so some daylight would be welcome. And, on top of that, it would be good to be able to see outside. It may have been paranoia, but before they entered, Mike was certain he had seen a familiar van pull into the street. The same one he had seen earlier. But he hadn't gotten a good enough look before Simon had opened the door, forcing him to act.

Before Mike had the chance, Kirsty spoke up.

'What is the mark on my back?' she asked, anger lacing her tone. She gave Simon a moment to answer, but instead, he just shook his head and pulled at his hair. Mike was worried the man was about to lose it and have a breakdown.

'I suggest you answer the lady,' Mike said, making a show of clenching his fists together.

Kirsty went on. 'I know about the Codex Gigas, and the missing pages.'

Mike saw Simon stop his manic fidgeting. The scrawny man looked over to Kirsty, with an expression of absolute shock on his face.

'How?' he simply asked, his nasal voice no more than a whisper.

'Doesn't matter,' Kirsty said. 'Is it true? By doing what you've done to me, have you tied some kind of spirit to me?'

Simon wrung his hands together, squeezing the fingers of one hand so tight that they started to go white. He nodded, but added, 'It isn't a spirit. Not really.'

'What do you mean?' Kirsty asked. 'What is it, then?'

'Something not from this world. Something that only knows evil and pain.'

Kirsty jumped to her feet and screamed, 'So why the fuck did you set it on me?'

Mike saw Simon wince again, and his crying only inten-sified. The man's face twisted up, mouth wet with saliva, and tears began to stream faster down his face. Mike had a hard time keeping up with what they were talking about, but decided to let it play out.

'I'm sorry,' he babbled. 'I didn't want to. I didn't have a choice.'

'Yes, you did,' Kirsty shot back, taking a step forward, her fists clenched. 'Of course you had a choice. You could have not broken into my home, not attacked me, and not set this fucking thing on me. Of course you had a choice.'

'I didn't!' he screamed, spitting flecks of saliva. 'If I don't tie it to someone else then it stays with me. It'll kill me and take my soul.'

Mike saw Kirsty stop in her tracks. 'What do you mean?' she asked. After a moment of crying and rocking, Simon began to pull off his t-shirt, to reveal a thin, almost emaci-ated body.

One covered with horrific scars and symbols.

Mike drew in a breath. He had seen what Simon had done to Kirsty's lower back, but this was on another level. Every inch of his torso was dominated by some kind of mark that had been cut into his skin, now visible as scar tissue. They stopped before reaching his shoulders and arms, so they couldn't be seen when he was wearing a top, but every-thing else was covered. Mike couldn't imagine the pain this man must have gone through when these were cut into him. Standing out most against the plethora of strange markings was the one in the centre of his chest—the largest one of all. It was similar to the mark Kirsty now had on her, but much more detailed, and instead of just having an inverted triangle at its centre, the concentric circles contained what looked to be a pentagram.

Simon angled his body, showing them all his back as well. That was just as bad.

'Why the hell would you do that to yourself?' Kirsty asked.

'I didn't!' Simon screamed again, showing his first hints of anger amongst his fear. It caused Kirsty to step back and Mike to immediately jump to his feet. Simon looked over to him, and the anger vanished. But Simon went on, 'I didn't do this. I didn't do any of it. I didn't ask for it, either.'

'So who did it?' Kirsty asked.

He again started to cry. 'Them,' he simply said. 'They did it when I was young. They summoned the thing, and bound it to me. Then they would attach it to others, some willingly, most not, to see what would happen. But it always came back to me. I managed to get away. I ran. Ran for my life. But the thing followed me. So I do what I have to do.'

Mike's head was spinning, and he felt like he had to step in and get some clarity on all the madness. 'What are you talking about, Simon? Who are these... *people*?'

'A group who follow the dark texts. They believe in another existence, one outside of our own. And they try to understand and contact this other place.'

'A cult,' Amanda said. 'You were in a cult.'

Simon just shrugged. 'I didn't ask to be in it. I was born into it. My parents were devoted members. They even offered me up to the elders, so that they could do this to me.' He waved a hand about the awful scars that covered his body.

'Your own parents did that to you?' Kirsty asked.

Simon nodded. 'They played a part. When I got the chance, I ran away. But I have to keep the thing they summoned occupied. If I don't offer others to it, then it will claim me.'

'So you'd happily let others die to save yourself,' Kirsty said.

Simon looked up to her through wet eyes. 'Wouldn't you?'

Kirsty paused for a moment, a little caught off guard. She then shook her head. 'No. No, I would never do that.'

Simon just let out a snort. 'I don't believe you. Anyone would do the same thing in my position, especially if you knew what happened after death.'

'And what does happen after death?' Kirsty asked.

'It takes you. Your soul. Takes it back to its home. It keeps you, uses you, and tortures you for eternity. There is no getting away. It will even use you to carry out its vile acts in this world, when it needs to. Like a spiritual puppet, dancing on its ethereal string.'

'Those are the others that I've seen following me,' Kirsty said. 'Those are its victims?'

Simon nodded. 'Before you, yes. They all went through the same thing.'

'And how many were killed because of you?'

Simon again shrugged. 'Not sure. I try not to remember.'

Mike saw a snarl form on Kirsty's lips. 'You miserable fucker,' she spat, then stepped forward and slapped Simon hard across the face.

Simon then kicked out a thrusting foot in response, forcing it directly into Kirsty's midsection and causing her to yell out and topple backward. As she did, she fell into Mike.

In an instant, Simon seemed to sense an opportunity and jumped to his feet. He ran for the door, fiddling with the lock, but Mike was up quickly, gently moving Kirsty out of the way, determined not to let the man escape.

Despite struggling to believe what he'd heard, he was

sure *something* was going on here, and Simon needed to be stopped.

Mike ran after Simon, who saw him coming and turned and scrambled up the stairs. Mike gave chase, hearing Amanda and Kirsty follow close behind. They all thundered to the top floor of the small house and pursued Simon into one of the rooms.

It looked to be a bedroom, but contained only a dirty mattress on the floor, half covered by some sheets, and an old wooden chest in one corner.

Simon turned, again pulling at his hair, a twisted look of anger and fear on his face. He was a trapped rat.

'That didn't get you far, did it?' Mike asked with his fists clenched.

'Just leave me alone!' Simon screamed. 'Please, just go away and leave me alone.' Kirsty pushed her way past Mike, and Amanda followed. Mike wasn't comfortable with that, given how Simon had lashed out, but knew that the girls needed more answers. So he stepped back, letting his frame fill the doorway. Unless Simon got to the only window in the room and jumped, there was no way out of here for him.

'Tell me how to stop it,' Kirsty said.

The man shook his head. 'You can't.'

'I don't believe you. Tell me. Do I just cut this symbol off? Strip the skin away? If that's what it takes, I'll do it. I'll just burn the fucking thing off me if I need to. The hell with the pain.'

'You can't!' Simon screamed. 'There is no way to stop it!'

Even as Simon spoke the words, Mike wasn't convinced. There was something in the man's eyes that gave him away.

'Tell me!' Kirsty screamed back.

Amanda joined in too. 'Just talk, you pathetic little fucker. Tell us what we need to know.'

Through all the yelling and commotion, Mike heard it too late: a creak on the floor behind him.

Then there was an explosion of pain in the back of his head. He felt his control of his body vanish as he dropped to the floor and his vision spun and blurred. Mike then felt his body twitch and writhe as he lay face down on the ground in a crumpled mess. The pain was extraordinary.

He knew he was dying.

27

Kirsty let out a scream after turning to see Mike on the floor. A pool of blood formed below his head, the crimson liquid streaming from a nasty-looking wound on the back of his skull, down the now glistening skin of his cranium to the dirty carpet below. His right hand was shaking, twitching, and a large man stood over him. The strange man was tall and broad and would have dwarfed Mike had Amanda's boyfriend been standing. In the man's right hand he held a hammer—the fat end smeared with Mike's blood.

Kirsty let out another scream as the man entered the room.

'No,' she heard Simon say from behind. 'How did you find me?'

The man just smiled and stepped aside. Three others entered, all looking thuggish and mean, and all with weapons of their own—two with knives, and one with a club of some kind. Finally, another man entered. This one was smartly dressed, with a shaped white beard. It was a person Kirsty recognised, only now the sinister smile he wore was far from the warm and generous one she had seen only a day before.

'Professor Beckett?' she asked, incredulous.

He laughed and stepped over Mike's now prone body. 'I'm afraid not, dear.' Kirsty turned to Amanda to see her friend staring wide-eyed at her fallen boyfriend. Kirsty had no idea if Mike was dead, or just unconscious.

'Brother Stevens,' Beckett said—or rather, the man who Kirsty had thought was Beckett. 'Could you finish the job with this man. We need to be certain.'

The large man with the hammer stepped closer to Mike and raised the deadly instrument above his head.

'No!' Amanda screamed, but the other men stood between them, stopping her from reaching Mike. The girls could only watch as the hammer fell, quickly and with savage force. It struck the back of Mike's head, sending out a sickening crack. Then it happened again and again. As the hammer raised back up, a long, red string of matter pulled up from Mike's skull with it. A final strike came down.

Both Kirsty and Amanda were in tears, and Amanda sank to her knees.

'How did you find me?' Simon repeated.

The man Kirsty had known as Beckett laughed again. 'With great difficulty, Simon. You've grown older, and you look much different. Not the young lad I remember. However, you have caused us a lot of trouble, do you know that? But deeds like yours, the things you have been doing since your escape, always leave a trail. I was able to learn about some of your past sacrifices—after they were dead, of course—and knew what you were up to, and that you were still alive. So I kept on looking, hoping to find a victim that was still alive, in the hopes it could lead to you.

'This brave girl here,' he motioned to Kirsty, 'posted on the internet, with a picture of the brand that you gave her. We have many of the Family monitoring for such things, hoping to find something. Yesterday, we got lucky. Kirsty here was marked, we knew, so we contacted her and gave her some details about what was going to happen to her. It was clear from what she said that things had already begun —much quicker than we had ever seen before—and we helped her to search her memories. To be fair, she did most of the work. After our call yesterday, we traced her address and got there as quickly as we could. Then, it was simply case of following her to see where she would go. There was no guarantee, and we had no idea if she could track you down, but like I say, we got lucky. And about time, too. We have been quite desperate to find you, Simon. You've been away from the Family for far too long.'

'You aren't my family,' Simon said through gritted teeth.

'Nonsense,' the older man said. 'Now stop this and come with us. Let's be clear, Simon, it isn't like you have a choice in the matter.'

'Who are you?' Kirsty demanded. She felt like her legs were about to give out beneath her. It was Simon Bridges who answered the question.

'Brother Ainsworth,' he said. 'He is one of them. One of the group. A lackey of the elders.'

Brother Ainsworth snarled, straightened up, and puffed out his chest. 'I am no lackey, you snivelling little brat. I am soon to be an elder myself. You best remember that.'

'So you aren't a professor?' Kirsty asked, stating the obvious. Ainsworth chuckled.

'Not officially, no. But I am an expert in my area of study, if that helps.'

'You lied to me,' Kirsty said.

'Yes,' Ainsworth answered as if it were the most obvious thing in the world. Not a trace of remorse. 'And you led me to Simon. I suppose I should thank you for that. You will have to come with us as well, of course. We will need to watch you, study what happens. Things seem to be moving very quickly; the entity must be growing with each soul claimed.'

'You aren't taking me anywhere,' Kirsty said. 'I've come here to put a stop to what's happening to me.'

Ainsworth laughed again, a condescending chuckle that rankled Kirsty. 'You don't have a say in this matter, my dear. Your fate is sealed. So why don't you make things easier and just come along quietly.'

'Not a chance,' Kirsty said. 'I'd die first.' She said it with such conviction that Kirsty surprised herself. Did she really mean it?

'Strong words,' Ainsworth said. 'I wonder if they are true? But there is something else you are forgetting.'

'And what's that?'

Ainsworth pointed to Amanda. 'Your friend over there. Are you as eager to condemn her to death as you are yourself? Because I can promise you, it will not be pretty. We will make you both suffer. So, what will it be? Come quietly, or are both of you destined die here and now?'

Kirsty took a step back, unsure of what to do. She looked to Amanda, who appeared as scared and frightened as she felt herself. Then Kirsty gazed down at the lifeless body of Mike; there was no question that this horrible man—this Brother Ainsworth—would follow through on his promise.

'Just let me go,' she said, but all the confidence was now gone from her voice. It sounded like she was begging. Which she probably was.

'Afraid not,' Ainsworth said, then turned to the pack of goons that accompanied him. 'I think we need to hurry this along, in case we've already drawn attention to ourselves. Bring these three along, please.'

He then left the room, and the four remaining men moved in. Kirsty and Amanda stepped back and soon found themselves standing shoulder to shoulder with Simon, something that didn't sit well with them.

'What do we do?' she asked Amanda.

'I don't know,' Amanda said, her voice shaking with fear. Tears streamed down her face. Kirsty didn't bother to ask Simon what his thoughts were, as she really didn't care what he had to say. However, what the man did next genuinely surprised her.

'I won't let you take me back there!' he screamed, showing a sudden aggression that Kirsty didn't think him capable of given the light she had seen him in today. He then ran at the men, bellowing out a roar, nasal though it was. He leapt at the man bearing the club... and was quickly swatted down to the ground with little effort.

Simon bounced off the floor and groaned as the back of his head struck the thin carpet and, before he could move again, Ainsworth's thug reached down and grabbed him by the throat. Simon was quickly and effortlessly hoisted up with one arm twisted around behind his back. He cried out in pain, but was hauled out of the room, shouting as he went.

'No, you can't do this. No. Please, let me go.'

His voice faded as he was taken downstairs, leaving Kirsty and Amanda alone with the other three men. They kept on advancing, and the tallest one—the one who had killed Mike—ran a tongue over his lips.

'We got the one we came for,' he said, 'but if you girls

want to give me a reason to get a little violent with you, you'd really be doing me a favour.' He laughed and grabbed at his genitals with his free hand. As he did, he let out what sounded like an authentic moan of pleasure.

Kirsty shuddered and tried to move farther back, but there was nowhere left to go. She pushed herself into the far wall, the mattress on the floor separating her and Amanda. The larger man, the one still rubbing his engorged groin, zoned in on her as the other two moved towards Amanda.

'Get away from me,' Amanda yelled, and Kirsty kicked out a foot to try and keep the large man ahead of her at bay. He just chuckled again, amused at her pitiful resistance.

'This is gonna be fun,' the large man said.

Kirsty and Amanda tried to put up a fight, but they were quickly overpowered and subdued. In the process, Kirsty took a few violent punches to the ribs, hard enough to make her think they may have been cracked, and both she and Amanda where hauled downstairs. They tried to scream as they were dragged away, but their mouths were quickly gagged and their hands tied behind their backs. Finally, burlap sacks were thrown over their heads.

Despite her wriggling and writhing, Kirsty felt herself lifted and dropped over a broad shoulder. She was then carried quickly from the house, the person holding her shaking her violently as he moved. The loud sound of a running engine surrounded her as Kirsty was then thrown to the floor of what she assumed to be a vehicle—likely a van, given the floor space she now lay on.

And soon, they were in motion.

Kirsty tried to scream for help, but all sound was muffled by the gag that was taped over her mouth.

She cried.

They had come here looking for answers, to find a way

to stop what was happening to her—but instead, Mike was dead, and she and Amanda were now in the process of being kidnapped.

Kirsty knew right then and there that she would soon be dead too.

28

Simon let himself sob as he lay on the dusty floor of the van. Bound and gagged, he could do nothing as Brother Ainsworth and the others took him back to that place they called home.

But it wasn't home to him, and never could be. It was only a place where insane people—who had tapped into a power beyond their understanding and control—gave their lives to worship at the feet of madness incarnate.

And some of those people, the most devoted, would give the lives of their own children, as well, just as his own parents had done—forfeiting Simon to the elders so that they could mark him with symbols from the lost pages. To summon that... thing, bind it to him, and condemn Simon to a life of torture and pain.

After a month of being kept as little more than an experiment, and suffering the horrors and abuse the entity brought with it, Simon's captors moved on to the next phase of their study. They took another victim, another teenager—this one the child of members who had transgressed—and marked him as well. Then they took Simon's blood and forced the boy to drink it. After the sickening ritual was complete, Simon was spared for a time—free of the horrors of the entity as it turned to another. The creature terrorised and tortured the other poor boy for years, finally taking his life.

And soul.

Then, the entity returned, only this time, it brought the boy with it, and Simon would often see his former friend's terrifying corpse, reanimated and intent on terrorising him. Then another was marked, and Simon again found reprieve. He was still a prisoner during this time, but at least he could enjoy a period of relative peace. However, he always knew the thing would return.

And it always did.

Simon was able to watch the procedure as the others were marked, and he studied what was happening, learning the ritual needed to move the demon on to another and away from him. The mark was to be cut into the skin of the chosen soul, which would prepare the body, making it ready to accept the entity and act as a host. Then the transfer was made, as Simon's own tainted blood was administered to the victim. Simon spent years, in the moments he had alone, drawing the symbol, leaning its intricacies, until he knew it by heart. The whole time, plotting his escape.

And escape he eventually did. He had hoped that distance from the Family would spare him, and maybe he could outrun the entity. But it returned, followed him, leaving him little choice. Simon knew what he had to do. The first time he marked a victim and forced his blood into them, it had almost gone horribly wrong. The girl was surprisingly strong and had nearly gotten away. In the end, blind luck played a part in his success, as she tripped and knocked herself unconscious. After that, he had a few years of reprieve before the entity returned for him, as it always did, forcing him to act again. The second time was simpler, and he quickly became comfortable and adept at drugging his victims, making his work easier. Over the years, he became better at making his attacks quick and clean, always working in the shadows.

But one thing he had noticed was that the entity started returning to him ever sooner and sooner, taking less time to claim the souls of its new victims. What would happen when it could not be sated by others anymore? What would become of him then?

Simon had a feeling now that he was being forced back to join the hated Family.

He continued to sob.

Andrew Ainsworth sat in the passenger seat of the van, constantly casting glances back to the three prisoners on the floor behind him. They were accompanied by three of the Family's most devoted members, and another sat up front with him, driving the vehicle.

Ainsworth contemplated taking a moment to relax, to enjoy the victory, but knew that would be irresponsible. This moment had been a long time coming, to be sure, but he was not over the line just yet, and he needed to handle the rest of the transfer with no slip-ups. After all, it was he who had been held responsible for Simon Bridges' escape all those years ago.

Not that he should have been, in his view, but that was what the elders had decreed. And that had put a sudden stop to his own ambitions of joining the higher ranks of the Family. Ainsworth had made some progress in the years that followed, but returning Simon Bridges would put right that past wrong. There would now be nothing standing in his way.

The secrets that his family had learned—the deepest, darkest knowledge that had kept many of the elders, including his own father, alive long after they should have died—would be his. He knew much already, things that most would not believe, but he wanted more. The pages from the Codex Gigas were a revelation to him—especially the passages showing that God, the Devil, and all deities humans had worshipped throughout history—were inaccurate, born from a truth that had been confused. There was no Heaven or Hell, only other planes of existence, where powerful, maddening entities dwelled. And some had found a way through here, lesser beings though they were... so far. It was the Family's responsibility to investigate the incidents and incursions, and gain all the knowledge and power that they could, so they could harness it. Ainsworth wanted to be the one at the forefront of it all, spearheading a new dawn.

And he was determined to make that happen.

But first, he needed to complete the task at hand. He had tracked Simon down, apprehended him, and in the process gained two additional subjects, one of whom was already marked, already a host to the dark entity from that other realm. They could study her; then, when her soul was taken, they could mark the blonde girl. The next victim was already lined up. It was perfect.

However, he had to get them all back to the village first, back to the sanctuary. Only then could he finally relax.

'How long?' he asked the driver.

'About forty more minutes, Mr. Ainsworth,' came the deep reply.

'Good. Drive steadily, we don't need to attract any attention. When we arrive, we will make the changeover.'

The driver just nodded in response and kept his concentration on the road. Ainsworth checked his phone and re-read the message he had received. The others were waiting for them.

It was growing dark, so they would have to be quick. Given what had happened back at the house, with one man already dead, Ainsworth had decided that they couldn't make the full journey in the van they were now in. They had to be smart, and cautious. If someone had notified the police and given them the registration plate number, then that could mean trouble. Thankfully, it was something Ainsworth had thought of ahead of time, and he'd arranged to make a transfer with a convoy of other members of the Family, before making the second leg of the trip. The van was disposable and would be torched at a location other members of the Family had advised: an abandoned farm out in the country. It was well hidden and quite private.

That farm was their destination now.

And soon, Ainsworth would be fully forgiven. Ascension to the rank of Elder would surely be his.

29

KIRSTY FOUGHT against whoever it was that dragged her from the van.

Minutes earlier, she had felt the vehicle pull to a stop and the engine shut off. Then someone had taken hold of her and dragged her from it.

The oppressive heat from the van was replaced with a welcome chill from the air outside. Given the drop in temperature and lack of light seeping its way through the burlap sack, Kirsty assumed that night had fallen. The sack was removed, showing her to be correct, and Kirsty quickly scanned the area, trying to figure out where she was. What she saw made an already terrifying situation much, much worse.

Kirsty found that she was surrounded by overgrown field and, in the far distance, could see signs of civilisation—streetlights and the tiny moving dots from car headlights—but they were miles away from her, making her feel much more isolated.

Amongst the sea of corn and grass was a large house, constructed of old looking-brick and a timber roof, one that sagged and seemed in desperate need of repair. Wooden shacks and outhouses, with corrugated tin roofs, dotted the land in the immediate vicinity of the oppressive house, leading Kirsty to believe they were on a farm, but not one that appeared to be inhabited.

Another van, this one black, and a few other cars were also parked nearby.

And, if the place she found herself in wasn't bad enough, the company that was waiting only made things worse. The large man who had earlier subdued Kirsty now held her fast, a huge hand tightly and painfully gripping her arm. Two others from the house had hold of Amanda, who was fighting to get away with no success. And then there was that man Ainsworth—whom she had known as Professor Beckett—walking away from them, along with the last goon from the house. Waiting for them, in front of the farmhouse, was some kind of welcome party. A dozen or so people, mostly men, were gathered. In some of their hands were flashlights, the only source of light other than the full moon above, and they cut through the night with sharp beams. There were no smiles or warm greetings to be had from these people, only stern, grey faces.

'So,' one man said, who appeared to be a similar age to Ainsworth. This man, however, was tall, over six feet, and stick thin. He stooped, with an obvious curve in the spine at his shoulders, and he had a long, grey face with dark eyes. 'You have him. And others, I see.'

'I do,' Ainsworth said, with a tinge of pride in his voice. 'Just as I said I would. When we have Simon back at the Sanctuary, we will once again be in control of the entity. And I'll be the first to tell my father of my success.'

'It is not a success yet,' the tall man said. 'And it was you who allowed this boy to escape in the first place. You still have much to make amends for, Brother Ainsworth.'

'But—' Ainsworth tried to answer back, though the man cut him off with a raised hand. This stranger then looked over to the thugs, who now held Kirsty, Amanda, and Simon.

'Bring them inside,' he said, turning to walk away. 'And someone dispose of that van. We must act fast and move again soon.'

'No one followed us,' Ainsworth said. 'Haste is important, but let us not make mistakes here. We have enough time.'

The man stopped in his tracks and waited, motionless for a moment, before turning back. He walked right up to Ainsworth, towering over the smaller man, and spoke, saying, 'Something *has* followed you, Brother. And I am disappointed that you do not realise it.' He raised a long finger towards Kirsty. 'She is the marked one, is she not?'

'Yes, but—'

The man again cut Ainsworth off. 'Then *it* is here with us, and we cannot control it in this place, which means every moment counts. Thinking that we have enough time is an arrogance that has seen you fail once before. I would have expected you to have learned from your mistakes. Speak to your father as you wish, but I do not feel you are ready—or worthy—of joining our ranks.'

Ainsworth scowled, but said nothing after being put squarely in his place. The tall man again turned and walked towards the house. The others followed, apart from two who made their way to the van Kirsty had just been dragged from. One of them held a canister, and Kirsty could hear the slosh of liquid inside.

Without further prompting, the man who held Kirsty

forced her forward, towards the farmstead as well. Amanda was dragged forward, too, and she fought and mumbled through the gag, but was ultimately helpless. Simon put up less of a fight, seemingly resigned to what was happening, a forlorn expression on his face.

The three of them were taken inside the house, along with the other members of this insane cult. As she crossed the threshold, a strong, musty smell hit Kirsty's nose—the air was thick with dust, and the hallway they stood in was dark, save for the beams from the flashlights, with no obvious power to speak of in the house. A side table stood bare—the only furniture present in the space—pressed up against the side of a wooden staircase. They were quickly forced left, into a large living area devoid of furniture, carpets, or even pictures on the wall. The only thing present, other than the gathering of people, was a dirty-looking stone fireplace on the far wall. It was this fireplace that Kirsty, Amanda, and Simon were pushed in front of, with the rest of the gathered crowd filling the remaining space in the room, cutting off the route to the door. A large bay window looked out over the front of the property, and Kirsty could see the two outside dousing the van in the liquid from the canister.

The tall man, seemingly the de-facto leader here, stepped forward towards Kirsty, and quickly yanked free her gag. Kirsty coughed and spluttered, taking in large gulps of the musty air.

'So,' the man said, looking down at her, his face unreadable. 'You are the one that is marked?'

Kirsty just scowled back. She was terrified, her heart racing and beating in her chest, but she did not want to show it. 'Fuck you,' she said.

He just smiled. 'Please, my dear, just answer my questions. Things will go a lot more smoothly for you if you do.'

Kirsty couldn't imagine what this man could possibly do to make things worse for her, given she had already been condemned to a fate worse than death. And now this man wanted compliance?

'I'm not telling you anything,' she said.

He simply looked over to the two men holding Amanda and drew out a large knife. It had a golden handle that was covered with carvings and markings. The man handed it to one of the thugs restraining Kirsty's best friend. 'Kill her,' he simply said.

The man took the knife and brought it to Amanda's throat.

'No,' Kirsty cried out. 'I'll tell you what you want to know.' She felt ashamed that she had acquiesced so quickly, but what could she do? Watch these men kill Amanda? The absolute best option available, meagre though it was, was to play for time and hope that some kind of opportunity presented itself.

The tall man let a sneer spread over his lips. 'Very good, my dear. Now, I ask again; you are the marked one, are you not?'

Kirsty nodded. 'Yes.'

'And you have seen the thing that is now bound to you?'

She cocked her head to the side. 'Not quite,' she replied.

'Explain.'

'I've known it was there, watching, but I have never seen it. Not properly. It was always hidden, either in shadow or just beyond my sight.'

The man nodded as if it all made sense to him. 'Quite right. In the pages, it is said that this being will not reveal itself fully, not until its host's final moments. I suspect you will see it soon, however. Now, what else have you seen?'

'Others,' Kirsty said. 'Men and women. Ghosts, I think.'

The man nodded again. 'Not quite ghosts, but it is as good a word as any, I suppose. They are a manifestation of the souls that now belong to the thing that haunts you. Twisted to do its bidding. Just as you will be.'

'So, ghosts,' Kirsty said, sarcastically. The man simply shook his head, as if disappointed with her. Kirsty went on: 'You know, when you talk like that, telling me how I'm going to die, you don't exactly make me want to tell you anything more.'

The man shrugged. 'I am only speaking the truth. How many times have you seen these things? How often do they reveal themselves?'

Kirsty thought about that. 'A few times. It started several days ago, after Simon attacked me and left me with that fucking mark. I've had about three experiences in that time.'

The man's eyebrows raised, and there were a few murmurs from those gathered. 'That is a lot in such a short span. Tell me, have you felt it yet? Has it, or any of its tortured souls, physically made contact?'

Kirsty nodded. 'Yes. With me, and her,' she said, nodding towards Amanda, mindful of the incident in the toilet. At the time, Amanda had sworn it was nothing, but now they knew better. However, after Kirsty spoke, the previous murmurs grew in volume and excitement. Kirsty noticed that Simon actually sagged in the grip of the person holding on to him, looking ashen. The tall man before Kirsty lifted his hand to silence everyone.

'That is troubling,' he said. 'If the entity is truly able to direct its energy to those that are not marked, then it is indeed growing in strength.' He then turned to Simon. 'Were you aware things had gone this far?'

With tears in his eyes, Simon shook his head. 'No.' His voice was soft and quiet, like that of a small boy.

The tall man turned back to Kirsty. 'I'm afraid, my dear, you do not have very long. A process that used to take years seems to have evolved quite rapidly.' He then turned to everyone else. 'Be vigilant, brothers. Time is now of the essence. We must get our new guests back to the Sanctuary, and quickly. But beware, things are more complicated than we first thought.' He then turned to Ainsworth. 'Something some of us should have considered beforehand.'

Ainsworth looked to the floor submissively, but even as he did, the bearded man's nostrils flared with anger.

Before anyone could move, however, a familiar sound rang out—familiar to Kirsty, at least. It seemed to seep out of the very air around them: a low, rumbling noise.

Something inhuman.

Then a breeze rose, slowly blowing round everyone crowded into the room, causing loose clothing to flap and flutter. The groaning sound grew louder, drowning out the panicked voices of the gathered cult members.

Kirsty felt her breath catch in her throat. She knew what was coming.

The tall man had said time was of the essence, but Kirsty knew that they were now out of time.

It was here.

30

THE TEMPERATURE around Amanda plummeted in an instant, to the extent that she saw her breath in the air ahead of her as goosebumps formed on the surface of her skin.

'It's coming,' someone yelled. A palpable feeling of anxiety rippled around the room and a few of the crowd gathered near the doorway backed towards the door, then turned and ran.

'Do not panic,' the tall, thin man yelled, a tone of authority lacing his voice. His followers wore their confusion on their faces—unsure as to what course of action to take: listen to their leader, or act on instinct and run. The guttural sound that had continued to build was now booming all around them, interspersed with thunderous banging noises, always coming in threes. The terrifying sounds were familiar to Amanda, reminding her of the previous night's events at Kirsty's home.

Then, another noise pierced the house—that of pained screaming and people in agony. Amanda looked to the doorway of the room, quickly realising that the sickening new cries were coming from the men who had fled the room.

Something was happening to them... something horrible.

Amanda was also certain that, amid the deafening sounds around her, she could make out a definite tearing and crunching coming from the hallway.

The room erupted into a panicked frenzy as a head, ripped off at the neck, rolled into view, the bloody stump leaving a trail of crimson liquid. The face of the poor man was locked in frozen horror as the cranium came to a stop in the doorway, in full view of everyone.

The crowd started backing towards Amanda, Kirsty, and Simon, pushing themselves as far away from the door as they could, and Amanda felt herself pinned up against the wall.

No... not the wall.

She felt a blast of cold air behind her, and a strong breath exhaled onto her neck. A pungent smell of rotten cabbage made her gag.

Someone in front of Amanda turned, obviously picking up on the same things as she had—a woman, somewhere in her forties, with greying brown hair. The look of terror on the woman's face only intensified as she looked past Amanda.

Behind her.

The woman screamed, alerting the others as well. The rest of them also cried out in fear, and as one they surged away from Amanda... and away from the thing that now grabbed her firmly about the arms with an icy grip.

'Amanda!' Kirsty screamed.

Amanda's heart raced, but in that instant she was too scared to move, knowing that she was being held by one of these... things. She looked down to see large, pale hands with blackened nails press its fingers into her flesh hard enough to draw blood. Amanda looked back to her friend as one of the hands released its grip.

In that instant, staring into the horrified eyes of Kirsty, Amanda knew this was the end.

'Kirsty...' was the only word she managed to get out. Before she could say more, one of those undead hands burst through her stomach, spraying gore onto the people before her. Amanda gurgled and looked down, seeing the hand that had penetrated through her very body flex its large fingers, rubbing the crimson-soaked tips together, as if the extremities could actually taste her blood. The arm then pulled itself free and allowed Amanda to drop to the floor.

She flailed around in a pool of her own blood, strangely aware of the sharp, coppery smell. The pain was overwhelming, as was the knowledge that she would soon die and, with the last of her strength, Amanda managed to roll onto her back and look up at the ghostly figure that stood over her. It was a woman, mutilated jaw ripped from her face, with ragged flesh exposed around the cheeks and upper neck. Her tongue writhed and moved and, despite the face having no mouth to speak of, Amanda could see it in her eyes—the demon above her seemed to be smiling.

That vision was the last thing Amanda saw before she died.

31

SEEING Amanda die before her very eyes was something Kirsty struggled to comprehend. As insane and unbelievable as the scenes around her were, the one and only thing Kirsty's brain was refusing to accept was that her friend was dead—now only a lifeless husk, staring up to the ceiling, mouth agape and a hole in her stomach.

And it was all Kirsty's fault.

The vile creature that was causing all of the torment and suffering was attached to Kirsty, and her alone. Despite the danger that had become apparent, Amanda had chosen to stay close to her friend and help, putting her own wellbeing in jeopardy in the process.

And it had cost Amanda her life.

It took Kirsty a few moments to realise that she was crying. Tears streamed down her face, and she let herself drop, falling into her friend's blood. She took Amanda's hand to find it was still warm. She then buried her face into Amanda's shoulder.

'I'm so sorry,' she sobbed, ignoring the chaos around her,

not caring what happened. Let the monster come for her and take her soul, torture her for eternity—she deserved it.

When Kirsty eventually did look back up and zone back into reality, what she saw shocked her.

It was a massacre.

The thing that had taken Amanda's life had moved into the crowd and was squeezing an unfortunate victim's throat, hard enough that blood and gore seeped between her fingers. But the spirit was not alone—others had now joined her, and they were all taking part in the orgy of violence.

Kirsty saw the ghastly looking woman that had climbed from under Kirsty's bed that night in the hospital, and she had her hands buried into someone's guts—smiling as the suffering man howled in agony. The spirit then pulled her bloody hands free, causing long, spaghetti-like entrails to follow.

There was also a boy, dressed in rags, with the same milky skin as the other horrors Kirsty had seen—he was mounted on top of a fallen woman—the one who had screamed just prior to Amanda's death—and his fingers were buried in her eyes as a gleeful, innocent smile drew across his face.

Other disgusting sights abounded as two of the men, in a blind panic, tried to break the glass of the bay window in the room. As they approached, a group of pale-skinned, naked figures made their way out of the swimming darkness beyond, standing on the other side of the window—entirely motionless, content only to block the way.

Movement to Kirsty's side caught her attention, and she saw that Simon was crouched next to her, eyes wide in terror, sweating profusely; but he looked poised, like a sprinter waiting for the gun.

He was going to make a run for it.

Kirsty felt a swell of anger bubble up from her gut. While she still felt very much responsible for what had happened to her friend, this man—this pitiful excuse for a human—was just as much to blame.

'You,' she said through gritted teeth. Simon's wide eyes flicked to look at her. 'This is all your fault.'

He turned away again, looking out through the carnage ahead. Kirsty knew that he was going to try to run, disappear without taking ownership of the misery and torture he was causing others.

She refused to let that happen.

He sprang to his feet and bolted into the crowd, but Kirsty was ready, and the second he moved, she did too, leaping over Amanda's prone body—skidding slightly in her friend's blood as she did—and giving chase.

As Simon moved, Kirsty saw that he nimbly bent down a few paces from where he had set off and scooped something up in the process. It was the knife that the tall, thin man had drawn previously. Kirsty didn't know where that man was now, likely lost somewhere in the chaos around them, but she didn't care.

Kirsty followed Simon's path as he weaved through the crowd, quick and weasel-like. As they moved, Kirsty was very much aware that, at any moment, a cold set of hands could grab her and end her life. But that didn't happen—the gathered horrors here seemed to pay the two of them no mind, concentrating on the others, enjoying the sick delights they indulged in.

Simon and Kirsty successfully broke through from the room and into the entrance hallway. Kirsty had expected him to make a break for the front door, but instead she saw him halt, turn, and then run up the stairs. Kirsty quickly saw why he had changed direction when she looked towards the entrance—more sentinels, standing in front of the closed door, eyes wide and a pile of bodies at their feet.

Kirsty thundered up the wooden stairs after Simon, determined not to let him escape again. She couldn't allow it —she was tired of letting people get away with the heinous things they had done to her.

At the head of the stairs, Simon ducked to his left, and she heard his footfalls echo down the hallway. Kirsty leapt to the top step herself and took the corner as quickly as she could, only to see that the hallway ahead was dark, very dark, with each door along it closed. She ran as fast as she could, trying to gain ground, and her feet slapped against the timber boarding beneath her as she did. Kirsty was still scared, but anger and determination overrode any hesitation that she may have had.

Simon reached the doorway at the end of the hall and rammed his shoulder into the door, forcing it open. Once inside the room, he turned and made eye contact with Kirsty. He tried to quickly shut the door, but Kirsty had made up a lot of ground and leapt into it herself, shoulder first, with enough momentum to push it back. Simon stumbled, and Kirsty was able to squeeze into the gap before he could recover. Aware that they could both still be followed, Kirsty slammed the door shut behind her.

'Leave me alone,' Simon yelled, brandishing the knife he had retrieved. 'Just leave me alone.'

Kirsty fiddled with the handle on the door and found a deadbolt, which she slid into place, hopefully holding off anyone that may have been coming up behind them. She then turned to face Simon, who was looking frantically around the room for an exit. But there was none. At least, not one immediately available.

They were in a bedroom, one that contained the wooden frame of an old bed—sans the mattress—and a thin and dusty rug in the centre of the room. The rest of the space, however, was bare. There was a single window; only this one was heavily barricaded with strips of old-looking timber boards. If Simon wanted to escape that way, he would have to remove the boarding, and that would take time.

Kirsty held up her hands, as if trying to calm a frightened animal. Which, when she thought about it, wasn't too far from the truth.

'Just listen to me,' she said. 'There's nowhere else for you to go. This is the end of the road.'

He held the knife higher, wrapping both hands around the handle, arms trembling. 'Don't come any closer,' he said.

Kirsty ignored him and took a slow step. 'Aren't you tired of all this? All this death?'

'What am I supposed to do about it?' he asked, voice still raised. 'None of this is my fault!'

'But it is, Simon. You didn't ask for it, I understand that, but you've kept it going, putting your life first and letting others die for you.'

'And why shouldn't I? You would do the same.'

Kirsty shook her head. 'I wouldn't. I couldn't let someone else suffer for my own benefit like that. And I think this is getting to you more than you think. But there is a way out, isn't there? You can end this, Simon. You can help me. And you know that, don't you?'

He shook his head, violently, and again pulled at his hair with his free hand, still holding the knife out before him to keep Kirsty at bay. 'No, there's no way to stop it. I can't help you.'

Kirsty could see through the lie. It was clear to her, now that she understood what was happening. The entity was currently tied to her, but she wasn't the original host. She wasn't the one who had bound the demon to their world. That was Simon. And it was he who could sever the connection.

But to do so, she knew, Simon had to die.

32

THE WEIGHT of the dead man atop Andrew Ainsworth was surprising, and it took effort to slither out from beneath him, but Ainsworth only did so when an opportunity presented itself. The violence around him—the slaughter of his brothers—had brought with it a fear like he had never known before. The Family dealt with things beyond human understanding, and Ainsworth had witnessed some terrifying scenes in his time—but the vision of his fellow believers being ripped apart by the entity and its minions, and the sheer power it possessed, shook him to his core. For the very first time, Ainsworth felt like he—and by extension, the Family—was no longer in control.

But there was a way out.

He had just seen Simon, and that wretched woman who was ruining everything, escape this room of death unscathed. He would follow suit, catch up to them, and make things right.

Ainsworth took a breath to steady his nerves, then pushed himself free of the weight on top of him. Just as he tried to move his legs, however, he felt something grab his right ankle, stopping his movement before it started. Ainsworth let out a scream and turned to look down the length of his body, expecting to see some tortured soul, some puppet of the demon they had summoned, holding on to him and ready to eviscerate his form. However, he saw something else—Walter Chambers, the tall man who, outside, had berated him in front of everyone. And Chambers, right now, was pulling himself across the floor, his long, grey face etched with pain and shock. The man tried to speak, but only managed to emit a gurgle and, as he did, a stream of blood flowed from his mouth. That was because the man's lower half was missing, torn off at the waist, with entrails and a section of spine dangling behind in a trail of glistening blood. With the last of his strength, Walter had clung to the only thing in reach—Ainsworth.

Andrew Ainsworth, however, scowled at the dying man. 'You deserve this,' he said through clenched teeth, 'for trying to hold me back. With you gone, there will be a place for me amongst the elders. Now, let go and die, you old fool.' Ainsworth then kicked his leg, shaking loose the grip of the dying man, and ran without looking back.

Avoiding the massacre, Ainsworth was able to make it out into the hallway, where some of his brethren had managed to escape to ahead of him. However, there were horrors in here too: evil and violent spirits that descended onto the fleeing men. One man's head had been crushed, one had his throat ripped out, and still another unfortunate brother's jaw had been removed by the apparitions.

Screaming in terror, Ainsworth was able to make it to the stairs and quickly climb them. He heard footsteps behind and, looking back, saw that three other members of the Family had managed to break free, too, and were following him up. Ainsworth continued to the top, barking out orders as he went. As scared as he was, Ainsworth could see a way through this. With Chambers gone, and most of the people here already dead, all he had to do was to get Simon Bridges back to the Sanctuary, and he could shape the story of what had happened in any way he wanted. Ainsworth was confident he could get any survivors to fall in line and back him up. After all, he was about to save their lives. The entity may be anchored to Simon, hence its existence in this world, but currently it was attached to Kirsty, and that was his window of opportunity.

'Follow me,' he said, short of breath. 'I promise you that we will live through this. What's more, we will go on to great things within the Family. Just listen to me and do what I say.'

They reached the top and turned into the dark corridor. All of the doors along it were closed, but Ainsworth could hear arguing voices from the one at the very end. Ainsworth turned to those with him and gave his order. 'Make sure Simon Bridges lives. But the girl... she has to die.'

Kʀɪsтʏ was still trying to calm Simon, but she knew that was a tall order given what she was going to try and convince him to do.

'Listen to me, Simon,' she said. 'I know you're scared, but you can stop this. I know the price is high, but just think about it. What sort of life do you have? Can you ever be anything but tired and scared? That's no way to live.'

'Stop it!' Simon shouted, and thrust the knife out at the air before him. 'I know what you're doing. It isn't going to work.'

'But I'm right,' Kirsty insisted. 'You know it. I'm not an expert in any of this, but I saw how shocked everyone was downstairs when they found out just how fast all of this was happening, and how quickly things with me had progressed. I saw how shocked *you* were. It's all speeding up, isn't it? So how long do you have left? How long until you can't get rid of this thing anymore, and it doesn't need another host? It can just take what it wants from those around you. That will be your life from now on, Simon. Either alone, with only that evil thing and its minions for company, or get close to people, then watch them die. Then again, it might just take you when it can.'

'Shut up! Shut up, shut up, shut up!' Simon said while shaking his head, his face twisted up in anguish. Kirsty had no idea how he was going to react if she kept pushing, but she had to try; there was no other option. What she was doing was horrible—she was trying to talk a man into killing himself, and what sort of monster would that make her if she were to keep going down that road? However, Kirsty knew—just as Simon did—that it was the only way to stop all of this madness. Because, even if Kirsty died here tonight and Simon lived, then it would all happen again to someone else. And considering what had happened downstairs, it also meant that many other people would die, just so Simon could live out a miserable existence for a little while longer. Kirsty genuinely felt that she wasn't doing this to save herself, but to stop it from happening again in the future, to someone else who didn't deserve it.

And, she was tired of being a victim, tired of others exerting their will over her and not caring what she wanted. The past few days had been terrifying and draining in equal measure—perhaps something the entity had desired—but it had also lit a fire in her belly. The events downstairs had shown her that things could be worse, and not just for her, but for others as well.

Enough.

It was time to make a stand.

'It's getting stronger, Simon,' she said. 'And that means, before too long, it will take you, too. Isn't that right?' He started to cry. Tears streamed down his face and his shoulders shook as Simon began to sob. It seemed that Kirsty was right, and this man knew it. He was cursed, and there was only one way it was going to end, unless he changed the outcome. Kirsty went on: 'So if this thing takes your soul, then you'll end up like the others, right? The other victims that it now owns and controls like puppets, that will be you. Tormented forever. Come on, Simon, there is a way to change that. I know it's hard, but if you do the right thing, then that creature will never own you. You'll end all of this on your own terms. You'll be free.'

Simon's shaking stopped, and his wet eyes softened.

Then Kirsty heard a violent rattle on the handle to the door of the room, which caused her to jump.

'Open up!' a voice commanded, and Kirsty recognised it as Ainsworth. The handle turned and jiggled again, but the lock held firm... for now.

Kirsty knew that she didn't have much time.

'Simon,' she urged, 'you have to hurry.'

34

'BREAK IT DOWN,' Ainsworth commanded. He didn't have time to persuade the girl or Simon to open up, and knew that they wouldn't listen anyway. Ainsworth moved aside, still aware that something else could follow them up here and attack, as the men with him began to kick the door in.

Ainsworth looked back down the dark corridor to the stairs behind them. The sounds from the level below—sounds that had previously been shrieks of pain and death—had grown quieter, now moans and murmurs. The massacre, it seemed, was drawing to a close. Which meant time was running out for them up here. With no more lives for them to take on the floor below them, Ainsworth knew that the entity and its puppets would soon follow up here.

'Be quick about it,' he added as the men continued to kick and strike at the door, aiming their blows at the area around the handle and latch. The door rattled in its hinges as they continued, one after the other, strike after strike. The largest among them then started to thrust his shoulder into it, throwing all of his weight behind his lunges. That finally yielded results, as the wood splintered and shunted back in the frame, now held by the last threads of the lock's resistance.

They would soon be through.

A child-like giggle from behind drew Ainsworth's attention. Reluctantly, he turned, and through the darkness ahead could see what was waiting for him: a group of apparitions, all standing stock-still with their pale, blotchy skin visible through the dark. At the front was the smallest one, a young boy who looked familiar to him. Behind the boy were others, including a woman with no jaw. None of the spectral figures moved at all and were mannequin-like in their stillness.

'Hurry, you fools!' Ainsworth shouted, now desperate. He heard the crash as the door gave way and turned to see that they were now through. Ainsworth knew that they had to kill the woman, and now, to stop all of the chaos before they died. Twisting his head back, Ainsworth saw that the group of spirits had now moved closer. They were still motionless, but their positions had shifted farther along the hallway.

The insidious things were all smiling now.

35

'WE DON'T HAVE any time left, Simon!' Kirsty shouted. 'You need to do the right thing. Please.'

But Simon Bridges was still in a state of conflict. He was crying, strings of saliva falling from his chin. Kirsty did feel for him, as he didn't deserve what had initially been thrust upon him, but he was a man now, responsible for his own actions, and those actions had cost others their lives in order to save his own.

Was that wrong?

Kirsty felt it was, but could she really judge? It certainly wasn't *fair*. But one thing she did know was that if Simon continued doing this, or if that fucking cult got hold of him again, then more innocent people were going to lose their lives.

And souls.

And that trumped everything else as far as Kirsty was concerned. She took another step forward, standing closer to Simon, but the knife was still aimed high, pointing at her throat.

'I'm scared,' Simon said, his voice a whisper.

'I know,' Kirsty replied. 'And that's okay. It's horrible what happened to you, and this whole thing is fucked up. But you have the chance to be brave and put things right. If you don't, it's not just others that will suffer. You know that. It's just a matter of time before that thing comes for you, as well.'

Simon continued to sob, but Kirsty saw something in his eyes. A look of realisation and, perhaps, acceptance. She gave him a sad smile.

'I'm sorry,' he said.

'It's okay,' she replied, relieved that she had finally gotten through to him. Simon then started to slowly turn the knife, away from Kirsty and on to himself.

A low growl erupted around them—the unnatural sound of the entity Kirsty now knew all too well, making itself known. The darkness in the room seemed to deepen and grow stronger. At that same moment, the door to the room finally gave way and the group of men, led by Ainsworth, piled inside.

36

'PUT THAT DOWN, SIMON!' Andrew Ainsworth commanded him. The old man had broken his way into the room, along with other members of the Family, and Simon had taken a step back. Kirsty, the girl he had been talking to, had made a lot of sense to Simon, as much as he hated to admit it.

'Leave him alone,' Kirsty yelled at them. She turned back to him. 'Don't let them tell you what to do anymore, Simon. Don't let them control you.'

'Silence, whore!' Ainsworth shouted.

Amongst it all, Simon could sense the air around him grow heavy and oppressive. Though there was no real light around them to extinguish, it actually seemed to be getting darker... and Simon knew what that meant.

Ainsworth's face fell as he heard the booming growls reverberate around the room. They were incomprehensible, inhuman noises, but Simon knew very well what they really were—the entity was speaking. It wasn't something the human ear could decipher, but Simon knew enough to realise that the demon would soon make itself known to them.

And that terrified him to his core.

'Don't listen to them, Simon,' Kirsty said again, and Simon saw the hair around her face flutter from a breeze that drifted in from an unknown origin.

'Simon,' Ainsworth snapped, 'ignore her.' Ainsworth then turned to the others who were with him. 'Go on, kill her. And be quick about it. That will buy us time enough to get him back home.'

Then men moved in towards Kirsty, who in turn backed up as much as she could. Simon couldn't organise his thoughts; there was just too much for him to dissect. The girl was trying to convince him to kill himself, Ainsworth wanted him as a prisoner, and the demon that had ruined his whole life was starting to show itself.

And speak to him.

'Don't move!' Simon shouted, putting the knife closer to his own throat. 'Nobody move! Just stop. All of you. Please, just shut up.'

'Simon, listen to me,' Ainsworth said.

'No,' Kirsty cut in. 'You need to listen to me!'

'Simon,' Ainsworth repeated, but Simon blocked out what he said next. It was all too much for him—too confusing. He felt an intense cold presence behind him, and that incessant growling suddenly became clear. A voice inside his mind, not his own, spoke to him, making him see sense, clearing away the confusion that had previously clouded his mind.

'Everyone shut up!' Simon screamed, loud enough that his throat hurt. 'Shut the fuck up.'

He was tired of it. Ainsworth just wanted to lock him up —trapped and caged, to be studied like a rat. Kirsty had confused him, momentarily, but she only wanted to save herself and let him die.

They were all trying to get inside his head for their own ends, to make him do what *they* wanted—what was best for *them*. None of them cared about him. So, he knew that he had to go back to what he knew best. It was the only chance he had.

Others appeared in the room with them, and some of these pale figures Simon recognised from back when they had been alive. Simon was the reason they had died in the first place. He had placed the curse upon them to save himself.

But you didn't have any choice, a voice said within, and Simon wasn't sure if it was his own, or that of something else. The voice went on. *Don't listen to the girl. She's trying to fool you. Do what you have to do.*

Simon lowered the knife away from his throat. He would not be tricked by her. Instead, he would use the knife on her and gut her like she deserved. The entity would then return to him, he knew, but was that really so bad? What if the demon could be reasoned with? That seemed to make sense to him.

Somewhere inside, he sensed something was wrong with that line of thinking, and part of him knew that he was being controlled... but at least that meant he would live on. He would survive, just as he always had.

On his own.

He looked to the girl and a sneer formed on his face. Simon readied himself to strike.

37

It all seemed to happen at once for Kirsty.

Screams rang out that cut to her bone; pained, shrill cries as the thugs who flanked Ainsworth were eviscerated. And that was the word for it, as the ghoulish forms that had materialised from the dark attacked the unprepared men.

Not that they could have ever been prepared for what came to them, of course. Limbs were torn off, a head turned to mush, and bodies torn apart. During the chaos, a sharp, coppery smell filled the air. Kirsty screamed as the violence exploded around her. She saw Ainsworth duck for cover as one of the pale forms moved over to him, drifting through the air, its head lolled to the side as it closed in. Ainsworth shrieked in terror, hands held up before his face.

When she turned back to Simon, she saw a different man than the one who had earlier been on the verge of listening to her. The guilt and acceptance that were there had been replaced by a look of grim determination, and the blade of the knife had turned away from his own throat and was now trained on her. Behind Simon, the shadows had darkened, and Kirsty could see movement and hear horrible sounds from within.

She knew what that was.

Simon stepped forward. 'You did all of this,' he said through gritted teeth. 'You brought all of it down on me. And then you wanted me to kill myself just to save your own skin. You selfish bitch! I won't do it!' He was screaming now, bearing down on her, knife held high. 'I'll kill you first!'

Kirsty took a step back as he moved towards her, noticing that Simon's eyes were now wide and manic. He wasn't the same person than he had been only moments before, and that terrified her. There would be no talking him down now. He intended to kill her.

Panic rose in her chest, and Kirsty felt fear grip her, threatening to render her immobile. There was no way out of this now. A madman was coming at her with a knife, impossible ghosts were tearing people apart, and the demon behind it all, the one pulling the strings, watched on from the deep black in the corner of the room.

Kirsty knew that there was no way she overcome all of that—she was helpless once again. Just like she had been with Dom, and then the night that Simon had attacked her. The victim yet again. She hated that she would die feeling powerless.

The tears that had threatened to fall now broke free as she realised that all of the bravery and grit she'd earlier mustered had been for naught. Kirsty tried to beg Simon to stop, but the words would just not form.

She felt pathetic, and her thoughts then ran to Amanda, her good friend, who lay dead on the floor downstairs. What would Amanda think of how quickly Kirsty had wilted? Amanda had always stood up for herself when she needed to, and even given her life, but that would be for nothing now as Kirsty had failed.

It all seemed so unfair to her, and Kirsty just wished none of this had ever happened to her—she wished that she could go back to the night in the pub, with all of her friends as they talked and laughed and fooled around as Amanda had shown her that stupid self—defence move. All in a warm, safe, and secure environment of their local pub. Then, afterwards, she could have just gone back to Amanda's and avoided all of the madness.

Hindsight was a hell of a thing.

'I'll kill you!' Simon screamed and pulled his arm back, ready to strike. Then Kirsty's mind suddenly focused on something, her memory of that particular night with her friends—a way to stand up for herself.

Simon lunged forward and, as he did, Kirsty readied herself, summoning every ounce of aggression and assertiveness she could. She let out a furious roar, then stepped into his attack, catching Simon off guard, and thrust her arms out, grabbing his wrist as hard as she could. Kirsty saw the surprise on his face and, with all the strength she had, she clumsily ducked under his arm and twisted it. Simon actually yelped out in shock as Kirsty forced his arm back on itself at the elbow, throwing her whole bodyweight behind the movement.

It all happened in an instant, and it was far from the graceful and fluid motion that Amanda had shown her, but it was enough to be successful.

Kirsty heard a wet squelch as the knife buried itself into Simon's gut.

He let out a surprised grunt and, for a moment, the two of them locked eyes—their faces now only inches apart. The anger fell away from his expression and was quickly replaced by sadness. He then looked down, and Kirsty followed his gaze. They both released their grip on the knife, which stayed in place, the handle protruding from his belly. A thunderous roar went up around them, powerful enough to shake the room, to the extent that some of the boards over the windows shook loose.

Simon wheezed and began to shake, and he then fell into Kirsty, who did her best to hold his weight and lower the wounded man down to the ground. He grabbed her arms, but she knew instantly that it was not an aggressive move—more like that of a child holding on to an adult for safety.

'No,' he gasped, panic evident in his voice. As much as Kirsty hated this man, she felt for him in that moment, and she tenderly took hold of his head and pulled it into her breast.

'It's okay,' she whispered to him.

Simon hugged her tightly. 'I didn't want any of this,' he said. 'I didn't want to hurt anyone.'

'I know,' Kirsty replied.

His breathing became slow and laboured. 'I don't want to die.'

The vibrations in the very air around them raised in ferocity as the ghostly apparitions advanced towards Kirsty; she looked up to see that all of the other men in the room—except for the cowering Ainsworth—were dead, their bodies now unrecognisable piles of mush. To her right, where Simon had stood only moments before, Kirsty saw something emerge from the darkness and make itself known.

38

As the ghostly woman drifted through the dark towards his fallen body, Andrew Ainsworth was certain he was going to die.

The spectre's head was dropped to one side, dark hair dangling down, allowing a clear view of her face. Wide eyes, complete with the symbol from the Codex Gigas etched into them, glinted in the darkness, and she had milky skin that was lined with deep purple veins. A gaping black hole where her throat should have been revealed itself further as she rolled her head back.

And Ainsworth could see what was happening to his brothers behind her—they were all dead, or close to it, destroyed by the terrifying beings he and his family had drawn forth from that other place.

Everything had gone wrong in the blink of an eye.

Where he had once thought he could right past wrongs and gain the position at the table he was owed, it now seemed certain he was going to die here in this wreck of a house, out in the middle of nowhere.

Not a worthy death for someone of his status and potential.

And perhaps the scariest thought to Ainsworth about the end of his existence, was that he would never know the deepest, most important secrets that his Family had come to learn over their centuries of existence, in all their different forms.

His life would end here, as that of a mere mortal.

With no knowledge of the hidden truths and eldritch wisdom he had been working towards.

Ainsworth held his hands up before his face and turned his head, braced for the pain that would come from the undead entity that moved towards him. As he turned his head, however, a thunderous growl rang out, and he saw Simon drop into the arms of that girl—the blade he had previously been holding now buried into his gut.

The floating woman before him then paused, becoming static in the air. Ainsworth's mind reeled, but he was able to piece together what had happened—and he knew that if Simon were to die here tonight, then all of his work would be undone.

The apparition that had been advancing was still motionless, still unmoving—paused with its arms outreached.

And that was an opportunity for him. Ainsworth quickly shuffled to the side, away from the thing that meant to destroy him, and got to his feet. As he did, ready to launch himself at the girl and protect that loathsome wretch Simon Bridges, he saw something emerge from the swimming shadows close to Simon and the girl.

And as it did, Ainsworth stopped dead.

The sight of the thing that emerged brought about a fear and panic within him that seized his heart—so terrifying and mind-shatteringly grotesque was it. He dropped to the ground, not quite able to comprehend the vile monstrosity that emerged from the black. His breathing became faltered, and each breath was a struggle as a sharp pain shot down his left arm.

Had the mere sight of this thing been enough to trigger a heart attack? Ainsworth rolled to his back, the only thing he was able to do.

He then heard the girl scream.

39

As KIRSTY GAZED upon the demon that emerged, she felt as if her blood had turned to ice in her veins. She had often wondered what the thing that stalked her from the shadows actually looked like in this world, but could never have imagined this drifting madness.

'Jesus Christ,' Simon muttered, his voice weak and raspy as he clung to the last of his life-force—blood spilling from his wound and wetting the hand Kirsty was using to support him.

Kirsty's heart pounded, racing almost to the point of failure, and her mind threatened to break merely from laying her eyes upon this horror. She knew instantly that she was about to lose her life and soul.

There could be no fighting this.

Simon squirmed in her embrace, pushing himself away from the demon, and Kirsty let him, shuffling herself back as well. Simon's moments were slow and laboured as he crawled, his skin now deathly white, and it was clear to Kirsty—even with no medical knowledge—that he did not have a lot of time left. Whatever damage the blade had done to his internal organs had been serious—seemingly piercing or cutting something of importance.

The air continued to get colder, and Kirsty's breath was beginning to burn in her chest. Her cheeks stung and fingers became numb—as if she had been out in the freezing cold for hours. The suddenness of the drop in temperature, one that only continued to worsen, should have been impossible.

Kirsty and Simon continued to move away from the living nightmare that stalked them. As it moved, it spoke, and the words echoed around the room. Though the sound didn't seem to originate from the grotesque form before her, instead coming from the very walls around them, Kirsty had no doubt it was the demon that was speaking.

'You will not die until I allow it.'

At first, Kirsty thought the statement was directed at her, but then Simon stopped and, with a groan of pain, rolled himself to his back.

'Keep moving,' Kirsty urged him, 'don't stop.' She didn't know why she suddenly cared about Simon or his safety, but it now seemed very important to her that he get away from this thing. Perhaps it was the same reason that she had held the man when he had realised he was going to die.

Whether Simon deserved what was happening to him or not, Kirsty was not a monster, and she was responsible for Simon's impending death.

'No,' he groaned, then added, 'no more running.' Simon slowly climbed to his feet, his whole body shaking as he did —stumbling a few times before finally finding a vertical base. Simon stood as straight as he could, still holding the handle of the knife. 'I'm tired of running. You won't control me anymore.'

A guttural laugh rumbled around them. Then the demon spoke a single, mocking word.

'*Wretch.*'

Kirsty watched on as Simon put both hands on the handle of the knife and, with a yell, pulled it from his stomach. An arc of blood sprayed out in its wake, and Simon wobbled on unsteady feet, but held his footing. 'I may be a wretch,' he said, 'but you won't take me.'

He then brought the bloodied blade up to his neck and —in one motion—pulled it across his throat. Dark red liquid spurted from the wound and Simon's eyes widened. The creature let out another bellowing, angry roar, and moved quicker than should have been possible. Its writhing form was on Simon before the man could even fall to his knees, and it wrapped around him, smothering him in its dark mass, engulfing him completely. Then, to Kirsty's eternal confusion, the thing began to dissipate from view, and the form of Simon, wavering as he held himself up on his knees, could once again be seen as the demon finally disappeared. It all happened so fast, Kirsty wasn't sure if the entity had just vanished, or had actually entered Simon's body.

Simon's eyes looked empty, glazed over, and blood still ran from the yawning pit in his neck. He then fell to his side, the blank expression never changing as he hit the floor, finally dead.

It took a moment for Kirsty, still shaking and terrified at what she had just witnessed, to let out a breath she didn't realise she had been holding. Kirsty looked at Simon's lifeless body as a pool of liquid began to form beneath his head, flowing from the deep, open wound across his throat.

The temperature in the freezing room soon began to normalise, lifting as quickly as it had dropped. Kirsty quickly turned to look around the rest of the room and saw that the other entities, the puppets of that demon, had vanished as well, leaving behind only the mangled remains of their victims.

And Ainsworth, who lay on his back, clutching his chest.

Was it over?

She looked back to Simon.

That nightmarish demon had enveloped the man before his death, but Kirsty wasn't sure what had happened to it. Perhaps it had been cast back to where it came from?

And what did that mean for Simon and his soul?

Kirsty slowly rose to her feet and, as she did, the overwhelming emotion of it all came to bear—crashing down on her like a physical weight. Recent memories flashed through her mind: the attack, the horrible things she had seen, and most of all, losing her best friend, Amanda.

Kirsty lost the vertical footing she had just gained, her legs giving out, and dropped down to her knees.

She began to cry.

40

She didn't know how long she stayed in that dark, horrific room, crying and sobbing—it could have been minutes, or hours, but eventually a realisation struck Kirsty: she needed to get out of that place. Regardless of what had just happened, with the demon seemingly disappearing, Kirsty still didn't know if the place was actually safe.

What if it wasn't over? What if some of the cultists downstairs had survived? Or what if more of them were to descend on this place to aid their brethren?

She needed to leave, and not just for herself—she couldn't let Amanda's body remain here. Kirsty needed to get back to civilisation and call the police so that they could come and collect her friend.

Yet again, with a renewed determination, Kirsty stood up. She turned and started to walk out of the room, past Ainsworth, who looked up at her as she walked, struggling to breathe.

'You'll pay for this,' he wheezed.

Kirsty stopped, then turned to face him. The threat did

not sit well with her. She walked close to him, then raised a foot.

'No,' she said, dropping it down hard onto his chest, 'I won't.'

Ainsworth let out a grunt of pain and his face began to redden. Kirsty applied more pressure, aware he was suffering from some kind of heart attack. She had no idea if it would be fatal or not, though she knew the pressure she was applying would certainly not be helping. But Kirsty didn't care about that, she didn't care if he lived or died, all she cared about was making herself clear to this worm of a man.

'I want you to listen to me, Mr. Ainsworth,' she said, 'and listen closely. It seems you're the last one left alive here, and from the looks of it, you aren't doing too well. If,' Kirsty pressed down harder, causing him to yelp, 'you manage to survive and get out of here, then I strongly advise you to leave me alone. If you don't, and you come for me, then I promise you I will gut you. That isn't an idle threat, either. I'm beyond tired of fuckers like you pushing me around. You're a worm, nothing more. So, if I see your face again, then things aren't going to end well for you. I do hope you believe me, as it might just save your life.'

He made as if to say something, but Kirsty cut it off by dropping more weight onto her foot. She twisted her shoe, making him groan and squirm even more.

'And now I'm going to walk out of here,' she went on. 'I'm going to take one of the cars out there and go to the police. I'm going to tell them that my friend and I were kidnapped and brought out here. The police will come, so you best pray you're able to pull yourself round enough to get away before that happens. If you do, I want you to disappear from my life for good. Now, do you understand everything I've just told you? You leave me alone forever, and I let you live. Understand?'

At first Ainsworth made no movement, and he simply glared up at Kirsty with his red face twisted in pain. Another sharp stamp on his chest caused him to shriek in agony, and he started to nod, quickly.

'I... understand,' he rasped.

'Good,' Kirsty said, finally taking her foot off of him. She looked down at Ainsworth, feeling a hate she'd never thought she was capable of—beyond what she had felt towards Simon, and even her ex-boyfriend Dom. Kirsty even thought about reaching down and strangling the very life from Ainsworth's body while she had the chance, though she knew she wouldn't. She wasn't like that man and his ilk. And she wouldn't let herself sink to their level.

Kirsty then turned and left the room, leaving Andrew Ainsworth to wheeze and moan, unsure if he would live or die, and uncaring either way. She made her way along the hallway and back down the stairs, where the remnants of the massacre that had taken place were on show. It was horrific, much worse than the mess left in the bedroom upstairs.

Through the glazed section of the front door, Kirsty could make out the orange glow of fire—the vehicle they'd arrived in was still ablaze. So, that meant she needed to take one of the others, and to do that she needed a key.

After taking a breath to steel herself, Kirsty began to pick through the remains, searching the pockets of the clothing. It was a disgusting task, but she forced herself to push on, and eventually found what she was looking for—a set of keys, tucked away in the breast pocket of a corpse without a head. Kirsty then quickly ran outside, finding the cold night air refreshing on her skin, helping to cool her. She could hear the crackling of the flames from the van that still burned, and had no idea if there was risk of the petrol tank catching fire and the vehicle exploding—so she was quick to find the car that corresponded to the keys she had.

After trying two—an SUV and small hatchback—she came upon the one she was looking for: an old model BMW that had seen better days. Kirsty hopped into the driver seat, started the engine—which, thankfully, rumbled to life on the first try—and readied herself to leave this place behind.

Before she did, she allowed herself one last look at the ramshackle house. Kirsty's plan was to go straight to the nearest police station, but she had no idea what she would tell them. The fact that she and her friend had been kidnapped, and her friend killed, was obvious, but should she also tell the police about this cult, and their involvement with Simon Bridges? And if so, how far did she go with it? The thought of telling anyone about the more... unnatural... elements of what had happened made her stomach knot up. There was no way anyone would believe her. Perhaps it would be better to hold some of the truth back? She sighed, deciding that she had time during the drive ahead to make up her mind.

And there were other things to consider, too.

The events of the night would leave a mark, one that would outlast the physical one on her back. Even if Kirsty was able to have the scar removed somehow, she could never forget what had happened here. To her, and to Amanda.

But Kirsty also knew that it didn't have to define her. She could live with it and grow.

She would be a victim no more.

Kirsty put the car in gear and drove away into the night, unsure as to what the future would bring.

41

SMALL CAPS Simon was terrified. After cutting his own throat, he should have lost consciousness and fallen into the eternal void of death, never to know anything ever again.

But that wasn't the case.

He now found himself in a terrifying hellscape, one that was hauntingly familiar to him. He had dreamed about this place, every night, for as long as he could remember. But to actually experience it was a completely new level of terror.

Simon was naked—his pale, blotchy skin exposed to the harsh winds that blew about him. The floor beneath his feet was a hard, harsh, black rock. It was solid, yet it excreted a thick, red liquid as his weight pressed down on it. The landscape before him was alien, with cylindrical towers in the distance shooting up in the sky, dwarfing the jagged mountains that lay between. The sight of creatures he could not comprehend, some as large as the very mountains they crawled across, caused Simon's breath to catch in his throat. In the seemingly endless sky above, pulsating stars hung in eternal space. They seemed to congeal together at a certain point, swirling about each other like a circular galaxy. No, that wasn't it—the form the mass took was more like an eye. Just looking at this cosmic iris caused his mind to fracture and break.

Simon closed his eyes and turned away, unable to look up any longer.

It was then that Simon realised something was very wrong with his throat and he could feel liquid spill down his front. He brought a hand up and felt the yawning opening as his fingers slipped inside, touching his own larynx as the blood continued to run freely. It was agony, and should have been enough to immobilise him and have him gasping for breath—yet here, breathing did not seem crucial. In addition, the scars on his body, cut into him by the Family, were also bleeding, pouring with a never-ending flow of crimson liquid.

Simon tried to remember the last moments of his life before waking here, and recalled the demon's sickening form encasing him, then invading his body.

Simon dropped to the floor, realisation dawning.

It had claimed him. Taken his soul, like those he had condemned before him. And now Simon was stuck here, forever.

'Hey,' he heard a voice say. It sounded quiet, echoey, like a distant whisper. Simon turned and saw the opening of a cave cut into a high, black wall before him. In the entrance of the cave, a naked woman stood. She had long, black hair, sunken skin, and a gaping hole in her neck, much like his own. She shouldn't have been able to talk, yet she did. As she carried on, he could see the inner workings of her throat move around, the stringy black chords working as needed. Her words sounded pained, yet they were clear enough. 'You might want to get in here before one of those things,' she pointed to a colossal creature that moved up the side of a mountain in the distance, 'come and get you. It's safe in here.'

He didn't know whether to trust this woman or not, and he realised that she seemed somehow familiar, but the thought of being out here, exposed to those nightmares roaming around, was horrifying. He didn't need to consider the offer for very long before he got to his feet and ran over to her. The girl turned and descended down a long tunnel, and he followed.

'Where are we going?' he asked her.

'Somewhere safe,' she said, moving quickly, clearly very practised at navigating the harsh ground. 'Too dangerous up there.'

As she traversed the cave, he managed to get a closer look at her back, where he saw a familiar marking. Simon was well into his descent before he realised who she was, as well as the last time he had seen her—just before carving that symbol into her skin, as she lay in her home, unconscious.

Simon stopped.

'Where are you taking me?' he asked, his voice echoing off the rock walls around them.

'Somewhere safe,' she repeated.

'You're lying.'

Simon expected the woman to try to convince him otherwise, but she simply shrugged. 'Go your own way, then. Good luck.' She turned and carried on.

Simon panicked, not wanting to be left alone in this hell. He realised that, as much as he was wary of the woman, he needed help here. Against his better judgement, he set off again, pushing himself to catch up to her as the tunnel opened out into an underground cavern of some sort.

The space was huge but the rock ceiling above them was

low, little more than ten feet high, which made the expanse seem oppressive, and a stream of black, bubbling liquid coursed across the middle of the area. Simon followed the woman to the centre of the space. 'Wait,' he called. Eventually, she did, stopping dead in her tracks, and she turned to face him—the expression on her face not a pleasant one.

'We've come far enough,' she said.

'Listen, I need you to help me—'

'Silence,' she said, cutting him off. 'You are here because *it* demanded you to be. You are like us now. And you belong to *it*. You are a prisoner, and your existence will not be pleasant.'

Others like the woman suddenly started to crawl out of the dark nooks and crannies of the cave system, and most of these damned souls were familiar to Simon—past victims, people he had condemned to his existence. They circled him and began to close in.

'Stay away,' he said, holding up his hands defensively.

But he had nowhere to go.

The woman pointed up to the ceiling of the cave, where he saw that terrifying thing, the entity behind it all, emerge from the very rock—seeping out of its surface. The demon's growl erupted in three sharp, booming blasts.

'We exist here, in this cave, until we are called upon!' the woman shouted.

'And where does that thing exist?' Simon asked, squatting down, trying to keep away from the forming madness above, but pointing up to the crawling mass.

'Here with us, where it is safe. Outside of these walls is dangerous for all of us, including our master. So we hide here, until we are needed and used.'

'You just live here, with that thing?' Simon shouted, as the entity boomed again. 'And it just leaves you alone?'

A chorus of chuckles rippled from the people gathered around him. 'It *never* leaves us alone,' the woman said.

Everyone then advanced again, closing in, overwhelming Simon.

'What's going on?' he cried as dozens of pairs of pale hands reached for him. 'What are you doing?'

'Getting revenge,' the woman said, digging her thumbs into his eyes. Simon screamed and shrieked in pain as he felt liquid run down his cheeks. 'Don't worry,' he heard the woman say, 'you can't die. But let me welcome you to hell.'

Simon couldn't see it happen as his skin was pulled from his bones, but the demon from the ceiling above descended down onto them all, covering them with its sprawling, writhing, torturous mass.

They all cried out in anguish as the suffering began.

THE END

THE DEMONIC

Read more Supernatural Horror from Lee Mountford

Years ago Danni Morgan ran away from her childhood home and vowed never to go back. It was a place of fear, pain and misery at the hands of an abusive father.

But now Danni's father is dead and she is forced to break her vow and return home—to lay his body to rest and face up to the ghosts of her past.

But Danni is about to realise that some ghosts are more real than others. And something beyond her understanding is waiting for her there, lurking in the shadows. An evil that intends to kill her family and claim her very soul.

Experience supernatural horror in the vein of THE CONJURING, INSIDIOUS and the legendary GHOST-

WATCH. THE DEMONIC will get under your skin, send chills down your spine and have you sleeping with the lights on!

Buy The Demonic now...

FOREST OF THE DAMNED

Read more Supernatural Horror from Lee Mountford

The Black Forest. A place of legend and folklore. A place where the souls of the dead never rest.

A group of paranormal researchers head to the isolated forest with the hopes of capturing something that has evaded them their whole careers: proof of life after death.

The forest soon promises to deliver an investigation beyond what they could have ever hoped for. But things take a turn for the sinister when one of the group disappears in the dead of the night.

Ghostly apparitions, disembodied voices and demonic things lurking in the darkness turn the adventure into a living nightmare. Will any of them escape with their lives, or will they all pay for not taking heed of the local legend?

And at the heart of it all, the evil Mother Sibbett waits, ready to show them what the afterlife really holds.

A supernatural horror novel that will resonate with fans of THE BLAIR WITCH PROJECT and THE RITUAL. After reading this terrifying story, you will never go down to the woods again...

Buy Forest of the Damned now...

HAUNTED: PERRON MANOR

A TERRIFYING HAUNTED HOUSE NOVEL.

Haunted: Perron Manor

Book 1 in the Haunted Series.

Sisters Sarah and Chloe inherit a house they could never have previously dreamed of owning. It seems too good to be true.

Shortly after they move in, however, the siblings start to notice strange things: horrible smells, sudden drops in temperature, as well as unexplainable sounds and feelings of being watched.

All of that is compounded when they find a study upstairs, filled with occult items and a strange book written in Latin.

Their experiences grow more frequent and more terrifying, building towards a heart-stopping climax where the sisters come face to face with the evil behind Perron Manor. Will they survive and save their very souls?

Buy Haunted: Perron Manor now.

THE EXTREME HORROR SERIES

Three stomach-churning horror novels in one volume.

Horror in the Woods – A group of friends are lost and hunted in the woods, pursued by a family of cannibals who are hungry for human flesh. Buy Horror in the Woods now.

Tormented – Insidious experiments are taking place at Arlington Asylum, and the helpless inmates are the test subjects. Buy Tormented now.

The Netherwell Horror – Looking for her brother after a troubling message, a journalist ends up in the strange fishing town of Netherwell Bay. There, she uncovers a plot by a sinister cult to bring about the end of days. Buy The Netherwell Horror now.

The Extreme Horror Collection collects the preceding novels in one volume. Buy it now, and strap in for three sickening tales that push the boundaries of horror.

The Extreme Horror Collection

FREE BOOK

Sign up to my mailing list for a free horror book...

Want more scary stories? Sign up to my mailing list and receive your free copy of *The Nightmare Collection - Vol 1* directly to your email address.

This novel-length short story collection is sure to have you sleeping with the lights on.

Sign up now.

www.leemountford.com

ABOUT THE AUTHOR

Lee Mountford is a horror author from the North-East of England. His first book, Horror in the Woods, was published in May 2017 to fantastic reviews, and his follow-up book, The Demonic, achieved Best Seller status in both Occult Horror and British Horror categories on Amazon.

He is a lifelong horror fan, much to the dismay of his amazing wife, Michelle, and his work is available in ebook, print and audiobook formats.

In August 2017 he and his wife welcomed their first daughter, Ella, into the world. In May 2019, their second daughter, Sophie, came along. Michelle is hoping the girls don't inherit their father's love of horror, but Lee has other ideas...

For more information
www.leemountford.com
leemountford01@googlemail.com

ACKNOWLEDGMENTS

Thanks first and foremost to my editor, Josiah Davis (http://www.jdbookservices.com), for such an amazing job.

The cover was supplied by Debbie at The Cover Collection (http://www.thecovercollection.com). I cannot recommend their work enough.

Thanks as well to fellow author—and guru extraordinaire—Iain Rob Wright for all of his fantastic advice and guidance. If you don't know who Iain is, remedy that now: http://www.iainrobwright.com. An amazing author with a brilliant body of work.

And the last thank you, as always, is the most important—to my amazing family. My wife, Michelle, and my daughters, Ella and Sophie—thank you for everything. You three are my world.

Made in the USA
Coppell, TX
01 November 2021